"Vikram, what's wrong?" Jackie asked, and reached out for him. Vikram recoiled at her touch.

"We can't," he said, almost to himself. "We mustn't – it's not right..."

"Vikram, I love you," Jackie said. "I never knew before now. You were always around, the boy next door; I could never appreciate what was always under my nose..."

"You're my best friend's girlfriend," Vikram said, and his voice was breaking with emotion. "Don't you see? There's no future for us."

Also in the Point Romance series

Look out for:

Love Triangle
Lorna Read

Secret Love
Sue Welford

Dream Ticket: *Blazing Kisses*
Amber Vane

Malibu Summer
Jane Claypool Miner

Point Romance

Ice Hot!

Robyn Turner

SCHOLASTIC

Scholastic Children's Books
Commonwealth House, 1-19 New Oxford Street,
London WC1A 1NU, UK
a division of Scholastic Ltd
London ~ New York ~ Toronto ~ Sydney ~ Auckland

First published by Scholastic Ltd, 1996

ISBN 0 590 13347 0

Typeset by TW Typesetting, Midsomer Norton, Avon
Printed by Cox & Wyman Ltd, Reading, Berks.

10 9 8 7 6 5 4 3 2

PART ONE

1

"I want to die!"

Jackie Taylor looked up indifferently, shading her pretty hazel eyes from the summer sun, and considered the good-looking boy who had just hopped out of the passenger seat of the battered old Mini Metro parked by the open-air café.

He was a little under six feet, which made him about four inches taller than Jackie, and was broad-shouldered and slim-waisted. His complexion was a light coffee colour, betraying his Asian parentage. He was wearing a baggy short-sleeved American baseball shirt (the Baltimore Orioles, although the closest he'd ever been to America was watching cops 'n' robbers shows on TV), a pair of jeans (torn at the left knee), and a pair of scuffed-up trainers which had once been trendy but now were just permanently muddy. A gym bag was slung casually over his shoulder.

"Say again, Vikram?" Jackie asked, and sipped at her cup of coffee.

"I want to die!" Vikram repeated, slightly put out that his declaration of wanting to end it all wasn't having the desired effect on his friend.

"Well, just don't do it here," Jackie quipped. "Not in front of Slinky Jo's, the trendiest caff in this part of the northern hemisphere: it'd get us all a terrible reputation."

She turned to her companion, a girl her own age, which was seventeen, whose short dark hair perfectly complemented her dark gypsyish eyes. "I tell you, Emma, some of these guys have no taste at all!"

Emma smiled, and pulled out a chair for the newcomer. He sat down, breathing out a long and heartfelt sigh of exhaustion.

"Leave Vik alone, Jackie," she said and laughed. She turned to the young Pakistani boy who was running his fingers through his thick black hair which he wore long and curly. Vikram was a year older than them, and when he had still been attending their sixth-form college he had had something of a reputation of being an all-round jock. If you needed to track down Vikram, so common knowledge had it, all you had do was go to the nearest gym or sports field, and there he'd be. Whether he spotted you there or not was another matter: when Vikram was playing sports or working out it seemed that nothing else mattered to him.

"So what were you working out at today, Superman?" Emma asked. "The London marathon or scaling the north face of the Eiger?"

Vikram grinned, revealing a set of perfectly

formed white teeth. "Nothing as easy as that, I'm afraid, just a game of five-a-side with Julian and the other guys down the park," he revealed. "But it's tired me out! I'm totally zonked!"

Jackie sighed mischievously. "I can't understand what all this fuss is about," she said mock-wearily. "Grown men kicking a piece of pig's bladder around the park. You'd think you'd have better things to do with your time."

Vikram smiled, and leant forward to give Jackie a friendly punch in the ribs. "And you will never ever understand, because it takes a man to appreciate the finer points of the noble and ancient art of good old-fashioned footie!"

"Chauvinist pig! Sometimes, Vik, you are such a stereotype!" Jackie joked, and smiled. It was a smile which lit up her entire face, making her by far the most attractive girl in the whole café. Jackie wasn't conventionally attractive, with a dimple in her chin which she hated, and long blonde hair which had a tendency to frizz at the ends if she didn't shampoo it sternly every other day; her beauty came from her naturalness and her open character.

Whereas other much prettier girls – and much plainer ones than her as well (Emma for example) – seemed to spend most of their time in front of their bedroom mirrors, Jackie rarely used make-up, and, although she did have one designer outfit, which she'd bought in the last January sales, she dressed mainly in casual, brightly-coloured sweatshirts and well-pressed jeans. It was a look which might have made other girls disappear in the crowd, but in Jackie's case it simply accentuated her happy-go-lucky personality.

"Anyway I haven't got anything better to do with my time," Vikram reminded her. "I've finished college now, and I'm taking a year off before I go on to university."

Jackie shuddered. She still had another year at sixth-form, but the prospect of anyone actually wanting to carry on studying for at least another three years, like Vikram, filled her with something approaching abject terror.

"And who's calling who a stereotype anyway, Ms Taylor?" Vikram riposted, when she told him this. "What are you going to do after A-levels? Find a rich man and marry him?"

Jackie pulled a face at her friend. "No way!" she said defiantly. "I'm not going to get married for ages yet. And when I do it'll be after I've made a career for myself. I'm going to marry for love, not money, and I'm not going to be some rich man's servant!"

"Just don't tell Julian that," Emma muttered under her breath, fortunately not quite loud enough for Jackie or Vikram to hear her.

"Besides I'm not clever enough to go to university like you," Jackie continued. "I'd never make the grades." Vikram silenced her with a finger pressed against her lips.

"Don't ever put yourself down, Jackie," he said, suddenly all serious. "You've got to believe in yourself in this life. I did. My dad did. When he first came to England from Karachi, he was poor. But he met my mum, and she gave him faith in his abilities. They worked hard, and now they run two small grocery shops. A perfect pair. You can do anything if you believe in yourself and your own talents."

Emma yawned theatrically and took a bite of her chocolate fudge cake: it was loaded with calories, but *hey, what the hell!* she thought.

"Puhhh-lease! We're on holiday! Can we leave all the philosophizing and life-affirmation and calorie-counting until later? The holidays are supposed to be fun! Heck, I might even fall in love!"

Both Jackie and Vikram laughed at Emma: she was always complaining about how overweight she was (in fact, like most girls with the same complaint, she was nothing of the sort) while at the same time scoffing copious amounts of all the fattening foods at Slinky Jo's.

"Just to make up for my being such an obnoxious male chauvinist, why don't I buy us all some more cappuccinos?" Vikram suggested, and winked at Emma. "I might even be able to stretch to some more chocolate fudge cake!" When Emma nodded eagerly, he stood up to enter the café and place his order.

"Make that a double espresso for me," Jackie said. "And easy on the cream on the cake: at least I'm watching the calories!"

"*You* don't have to," Emma said pointedly, and gazed jealously at Jackie's slim figure. No matter how much Jackie ate she never seemed to put on a single unwanted ounce; whereas Emma only had to look at a Häagen-Dazs ad on the TV and it was Fat City all over again!

Resigning herself to the fact she'd never attain supermodel proportions so she might as well keep on scoffing her cakes, Emma glanced up to see a tall sandy-blond-haired boy just locking the door on the driver's seat of a Metro. She waved to him and beckoned him over.

"Three cappuccinos and one double espresso it is then," Vikram said when he saw the newcomer approaching them, and he disappeared into the café.

"Hi, Julian," Emma said, and asked the couple on the table next to them if they could take their other chair. She dragged the chair over next to hers, and then moved places so that Julian could sit next to Jackie.

Julian gave Emma a friendly peck on the cheek, and then kissed Jackie full on the lips. He reached out for her hand under the table and held it; his touch was firm and manly but as he stroked her fingers, Jackie coloured slightly and turned. Recently she'd been wishing more and more that Julian wouldn't express his affection for her in public so much, and she wondered why; last Easter she certainly hadn't minded when he had held her tightly all night at the end-of-term dance like he'd never let her go ("I thought you'd never come up for air!" Emma had teased her the following day. "Who says that you need oxygen anyway?").

Jackie watched a couple of good-looking Italian boys she vaguely knew wolf-whistle at a pair of girls walking down the street. The girls tittered, and the boys hurried after them, all Latin charm and flirtatiousness. Jackie smiled: it seemed like all four of them were having fun. At least they were sure of having a good time this summer!

"You're late," she gently reproved her boyfriend, and looked at her watch (a limited-edition Swatch which was his birthday present to her last year). "We'd arranged to meet half an hour ago. Did yours and Vik's match go on longer than expected?"

Julian smiled and took his hand from Jackie's and reached into the top pocket of his MA1 flying jacket. He pulled out a cassette and handed it to Jackie. She inspected the cover: it was the latest album by Powerhouse, the hottest band at the moment, whose last single had shot straight to Number One in the charts.

"I knew you wanted it," Julian said and flashed that eager-to-please, little-boy smile which made half of the girls at their sixth-form college swoon with pleasure. His sandy-blond hair flopped over his brilliantly blue eyes making him look even more adorable than usual. "So I drove into town after the game to buy it for you."

Jackie kissed Julian on the cheek. It was soft and smooth, unlike Vikram's, who even at two o'clock in the afternoon sported five o'clock designer stubble. Some of Jackie's girlfriends had said that it made Vikram look dangerously sexy, but she couldn't see it herself somehow. She'd known Vik for years: how could someone like him ever be thought of as sexy?

"That's so sweet of you, Jules," she said. "But you shouldn't have. You shouldn't spend so much money on me."

Julian shrugged. "What does it matter?" he

asked, and looked lovingly into his girlfriend's eyes. "Nothing's too much for my little girl..."

"Yuk!" said Emma, who feared that Julian and Jackie were going to indulge in some serious soppiness right in front of her and her chocolate fudge cake.

"Anyway, you know my dad gives me a bigger than usual allowance," he said, and glanced over at the Metro. "He bought me that for my seventeenth birthday last year; he's got so much money he doesn't know what to do with it."

Jackie nodded: what Julian was saying was right. Her boyfriend lived in the big house at the top of the hill with his father who was a successful businessman, and owned a string of fast-food hamburger joints across this part of the country. The weekly pocket money he gave Julian was four times what Jackie's hard-pressed mother could scrape together for her for an entire month. Jackie suspected that Julian's father's generosity was merely a way of assuaging his guilty conscience, to make up for his messy divorce from Julian's mother.

Julian had treated Jackie to unexpected presents ever since they had started going out with each other two years ago, when she was fifteen and he was sixteen. At first she had been delighted by his gifts, but more and more now she was feeling slightly awkward about accepting them. And she wasn't entirely sure why.

"It's really very, very sweet of you, Jules," she repeated, as she read the list of song titles on the back of the cassette. "But I was planning on buying this for myself later... Emma and I have to go into town anyway to see if we can find any Saturday work. I can't expect my mum to keep on supporting me for ever, you know..."

"You don't need a Saturday job," Julian reassured her, and draped his arm over her shoulder in what was almost a protective gesture. "I get enough money to pay for both of us to go out clubbing and partying... And if I run short Dad will always give me some more."

"That's not the point, Jules," Jackie said weakly.

"So what's the big deal then?" Julian asked, not understanding what was troubling Jackie, although it was obvious that something was.

Jackie smiled. "It's nothing, Jules," she said finally. "Thanks again – it was a really nice thought."

"Don't I get another thank-you kiss then?" Julian pouted childishly, his blue eyes twinkling mischievously in his fair-complexioned face.

"Of course you do," Jackie said, and kissed him gratefully on the cheek again.

"Besides," Julian said, and suddenly looked guilty, "It's a sort of way of saying 'sorry' in advance..."

"Sorry?" Jackie asked and frowned. "What for?"

Julian looked around sheepishly, unwilling to look his girlfriend directly in the eyes. He peered back into the interior of Slinky Jo's. Vikram was there, waiting by the counter for his order to be completed, and chatting to a good-looking brunette, who, in her tight red satin T-shirt and close-fitting designer jeans seemed as slinky as the café's owner (Jo, or Josephine) claimed to have been back in the seventies when she had first set up her business. It was just like Vikram to end up chatting to the sexiest girl in the entire café, Julian thought.

Well, the sexiest girl apart from Jackie, that is, he hastily corrected himself.

"Sorry?" he heard Jackie say again. "Sorry for what?"

Julian turned back to Jackie. "For standing you up tonight," he said finally. "It looks as though I won't be able to make it after all..."

Jackie's face fell. "But Julian, you promised you'd drive me out into the country," she said, her voice full of disappointment, as well as a dangerous touch of anger. "I wanted to have a quiet chat with you, maybe at some nice country pub... It was important to me..."

"No can do," Julian said. "A friend of Dad's is coming round tonight – some important person in the medical faculty at the local university. You know I want to study medicine next year if my grades are good enough – maybe he can give me some advice."

"But that's in almost a year's time!" Jackie protested. "You haven't even taken A-levels yet!"

"It's important," he insisted.

Jackie allowed herself the luxury of a childish little sulk. "This is the second time you've cancelled a date in two weeks, Jules!" she reminded him.

"I know," he admitted, and there was a genuine note of regret in his voice. "But I made it up to you, didn't I?"

Jackie nodded. "That new blouse was really nice – I wouldn't have been able to afford it by myself, that's for sure. But it's not your presents I want, Jules, it's *you*. I was so looking forward to going out with you tonight."

Julian brought his hand to Jackie's face, and turned it so she was looking deep into his eyes. "I really am sorry, you know," he said, and Jackie could tell from his expression that he really meant it. "And I'll make it up to you – maybe buy you that dress you saw in that classy store the other day, or take you out for a real slap-up, dress-up meal..."

"But tonight was going to be *my* treat," Jackie said. "I wanted to..."

"Wanted to what?" Now it was Julian's turn to frown.

Jackie shook her head. "It doesn't matter now," she said, and smiled half-heartedly. "Of course, I understand. It's to do with your career and that's what really matters..."

Julian smiled and kissed her again. "I'm glad you understand: I'm really lucky to have you, Jackie," he said, and left the table to go and help Vikram with the four coffees.

Vikram was still talking to the sexy number in the tight jeans, and she smiled appreciatively when she saw Julian approach them, as if, when faced with two such good-looking boys, she didn't know which one to choose.

I should have such luck! Emma thought and finished the last of her cake. She looked sympathetically at Jackie who, after a slight twinge of jealousy at seeing the stranger eye up her boyfriend, had returned to her coffee.

"Men, huh?" she said, impressing upon those two syllables a whole world of meaning.

"Why does he never think of me?" Jackie asked, slightly petulantly. "Why does he always have to put his career first?"

Emma reached out for Jackie's hand. "You know how tough it is to get into medical school," she said. "Julian studies every hour God sends him but he's still going to need all the help he can get..."

"Sure... I guess you're right..." Jackie said, and looked back into the café. Vikram and Julian were still talking and joking with the sexy brunette at the counter. Jackie thought that the two boys were enjoying themselves just a little too much.

"And besides you can't say he isn't sorry – and he always tries to make it up to you," Emma said. "He's always giving you presents – even when he doesn't stand you up! I wish I had a boyfriend like that." She considered the matter for a moment, before adding glumly: "Come to think of it, I wish I had a boyfriend..."

Jackie smiled, used by now to Emma's regular tale of woe. "You'll find a nice boy one day," she promised her. "And you'll find one when you least expect it!"

"With competition like that girl in there?" Emma asked, nodding over to the girl inside Slinky Jo's. "Do us a favour, Jackie!"

"You shouldn't put yourself down," Jackie said, unconsciously echoing Vikram's earlier words to her. "You're as good as any number of brainless bimbos like her..."

"She's slim, and I'm fat –"

"You're not fat!"

"She wears masses of expensive clothes, and jewellery, and looks as though she's just stepped right out of a copy of *Vogue*," Emma protested.

"Looks aren't everything, Em," Jackie told her. "It's what a person is deep down that really counts."

"It's still really annoying when you have to turn down party invites because you've got no boy-friend to accompany you," said Emma, "and you know that everyone else at the party is going to be on the arm of some sizzling hunk!"

"Don't be silly, Em," Jackie reproved her. "We've got lots of friends who go to parties by themselves, or with their other girlfriends. It's the 1990s, you know! We don't have to have a mere male to escort us everywhere!"

"Yeah, but the trouble is that they decided to leave their boyfriends at home," Emma carried on, indulging in a spot of self-pity. "At least they have the choice!"

"You've got Vikram," Jackie reminded her. "You like going to parties with him – you told me as much the other week."

"But it's not the same," Emma said. "Vikram's a friend, my mate, he's not my boyfriend. And the moment we arrive at the party, and the other girls cotton on to that fact, they're all over him, like bees around a honeypot, leaving me to play goose-berry!"

Jackie looked at Vikram who was trying to carry two cups of coffee in each hand, while Julian continued chatting to the bimbo. For the moment her jealousy of the other girl was forgotten and she considered Vikram, as he concentrated hard on not spilling any coffee, licking his lips, like a little boy performing a particularly tricky task.

"Vikram?" she gasped in astonishment. "Why would all the girls want to talk to Vikram?"

Emma raised her eyes heavenwards: Jackie was a lot smarter than she liked to believe, but there were times when she could be just so dumb!

"In case you haven't noticed – and from that look of pure amazement on your face, Jackie Taylor, it seems that you haven't – Vikram is one of the best-looking boys in town. Dark-eyed, moody with it, and he's got a body to die for! And I should know – I've been swimming with him down at the leisure centre."

"It's all those sports he plays, I suppose," Jackie decided, and watched Vikram as he weaved his way through the crowd of trendies standing outside the café drinking their coffees, or knocking back their bottles of Mexican beer.

"You mean the girls all find him really good-looking?" she asked and chuckled when Emma nodded her head. "When I look at him all I can see is that spotty and snotty-nosed little kid I used to play with when I was young, and he and his parents had just moved into our road. Or the young teenager who always came round to help me with my homework. I can't really imagine anyone finding my next-door neighbour sexy!"

"Huh-huh," Emma said. "Our Vik has quite a fan club of love-hungry females. Not that it does them any good!"

"What d'you mean?" Jackie asked.

"By the end of the evening, instead of being in a corner snogging away with some stunner from out of town, you're more likely to find him in a corner with a couple of cans of cheap cider, watching the late-night football or volleyball results on the telly with a couple of mates," Emma revealed. "Vik is strictly not interested in going out with girls: all he's bothered about is sport, sport and more sport!"

"They must hate him for that," Jackie chuckled, as she gained a new perspective on Vikram. She realized that ever since she'd been going out with Julian she'd neglected her other friends: she couldn't remember the last time she'd been out on her own to a party with Vikram or Emma... They used to have so much fun, and at the end of the night Vikram had always made sure that she got home safely, walking her to her door. She remembered that someone had once teased her about Vikram only walking her home so that he could steal a goodnight kiss; at which point she had exploded in a fit of giggles. *Vikram? A goodnight kiss? Oh, come on!*

"It's a challenge, I guess, and it certainly doesn't stop them trying," Emma said. "If I had a penny for every time some girl's asked me to fix her up with Vik, I wouldn't have to keep reminding my mum to buy a Lottery ticket every week!"

"I don't need a Lottery ticket when I've got Julian," Jackie said wryly, returning to the original subject of their conversation.

"Like I said, you're a lucky girl."

Jackie smiled. "I just wish he'd let me pay for things sometimes," she said wistfully.

"He's got more dosh than you," Emma reminded her practically. "And he likes to buy you things."

"He's been buying me more and more presents lately," Jackie said thoughtfully. "I'd just like to be a bit more independent, and not have to rely on him all the time. It would be really nice for him to let me look after him for a change, and not always have it the other way around. Sometimes I don't even think he needs me apart from as an excuse to spend his dad's money..."

"Never look a gift horse in the mouth," was Emma's cynical reply, although she detected a change in her friend's mood. Jackie's lips were trembling slightly, and there was a faraway look in her eyes.

"That's why tonight was so important," Jackie said. "I was going to pay for the whole meal myself – and we were going to go to a restaurant or a country pub of my choosing, and not one of the swish places he takes me. You see, Emma, for tonight only, I wanted it to be me who was in control..."

"In control? What do you mean, Jackie?" asked Emma, but before Jackie could answer Vikram had returned with the four coffees. He placed them on the table, almost spilling the contents of one as he did so. Jackie smiled, and just hoped that when, and if, Vikram managed to get a temporary job for his year off, as he wanted, it wouldn't be as a waiter in a restaurant: he was so clumsy that he wouldn't last five seconds before accidentally spilling a bowl of spaghetti down some swanky diner's best suit!

"A cappuccino and a double espresso for the two most beautiful women in the world!" he announced grandly, and sat down.

"Liar," said Jackie.

"Julian will be bringing the cakes over in a minute," Vikram told them.

"If he can drag himself away from that bimbo over there, that is," Emma said lightly. By the bar Julian and the girl were still getting on like a house on fire. (Or, as the cynical Emma might have put it, like a Black Widow spider selecting her mate.)

Vikram looked urgently over at Jackie. "Hey, don't get the wrong end of the stick," he said anxiously. "They're only talking."

"I wasn't worried," Jackie said, and at least sounded as though she meant it. After all, they had known each other for so long that she knew there was no danger of Julian going off with the first girl to come on to him. He loved her; otherwise why was he always spending so much money on her?

"I think Vik's just worried that you're going to throw a wobbly like you did last Christmas!" Emma said mischievously.

"I did not 'throw a wobbly', as you put it!" Jackie retorted. It was a sore subject for Jackie and one which she didn't like being reminded of too often. She and Julian had been at a Christmas party at a flat owned by some students at the local tech, when one of the students had come on to Julian in no uncertain manner. Even though Julian had managed to escape the girl's advances, Jackie had seen red, and it had taken all of Emma's reasonable words to calm her down.

"On past form I'd've thought you'd be over there by now, pouring several gallons of espresso down her front," Emma teased, and was taken aback when Jackie suddenly flared up.

"That's enough, Em! OK?"

"Sorry..."

"No, I'm sorry for snapping at you," Jackie said, and started to toy with her teaspoon.

Vikram looked curiously at Jackie, and then continued. "You shouldn't really worry, Jackie. Her name's Linsey and she goes to the tech down the road from your sixth-form," he said. "I've met her once or twice before, at parties. She seems to be a really nice girl –"

"And really sexy too," Emma added. "Or do you mean to say that you hadn't noticed?"

"Is she?" asked Vikram, and looked at Linsey again. "Yeah, I suppose she is kinda attractive ... in a brash and blatant sort of way ... and I guess if you like that sort of thing..."

Emma gave Jackie a knowing, all-girls-together wink which said: *See! What did I tell you!*

"Anyway, she said she knows this job that's going for the next six months," Vikram said. "It could be just what I need to earn some money before I go off to university."

"Vik, that's great!" said Em, and hugged her

friend. Jackie congratulated him as well. "What is it?"

"Nothing special," Vikram told them. "It's working in a café-bar, serving food and drinks."

(Jackie groaned inwardly: it looked like Vikram had found himself a job as a waiter after all!)

"Where is it then?" she asked anxiously, as worrying visions of Vikram dropping bottles of expensive vintage wines, and knocking over the dessert trolley, came flooding, unbidden, into her mind.

"Down at Blades," he informed her.

"Blades?" she asked. "The ice-skating rink?"

"That's right," he said. "They need someone behind the counter to serve teas and sandwiches – that kind of thing."

(Jackie breathed a silent sigh of relief: it seemed that the diners of England were safe for the time being!)

"Vik, that is the most wonderful piece of news I've heard all day!" Emma said, and clapped her hands together for joy. "It looks like this summer is going to be worthwhile after all!"

Vikram laughed at Emma's enthusiasm, and raised his hands, palms-outwards, in a calming gesture. "Hey, I haven't got the job yet," he reminded them. "I've still got to go for an interview later this afternoon!"

"Of course you'll get the job – after all, you're one of my best friends, aren't you?" Emma said confidently, as if that dubious honour automatically equipped him for any task under the sun.

"I'm sure you'll wow them with your charms,

Vik," Jackie said, and patted his hand encouragingly. It felt strong and warm and the hairs on it bristled at her touch.

"Thanks, Jackie," Vikram said, and smiled, before turning back to Emma. "But what's the big deal, Em? Why are you so excited?"

"Well, with you working as a member of staff we'll all be able to get in free every day, won't we?" she said.

"Hey, I'm not so sure about that..."

"Of course, we will," Emma said confidently. "I've seen the old dragon who runs the place – one flash of those sexy dark eyes and she'll be putty in your hands! You know Jackie and I love to ice-skate. And besides –" here she winked at Jackie – "think of all those men we'll get to meet!"

Jackie laughed. For someone who had never had a proper boyfriend in her life, Emma certainly thought about the subject an awful lot! She was about to say something when Julian returned, balancing four plates of Slinky Jo's famous chocolate fudge cake.

"Been having fun with your new friend?" joked Jackie, and gestured at Linsey by the counter: she was alone now and sipping thoughtfully on a glass of Diet Coke. She wouldn't be alone for much longer, Jackie realized, as she watched a couple of boys eyeing her up and moving in for the kill. From the looks of Linsey, thought Jackie, were those two boys ever in for a surprise! She looked as if she could eat them for breakfast and still have room for seconds!

Julian's face fell. "Hey, you didn't think that I..."

he began guiltily, but Jackie just sighed – sometimes Julian could take things so seriously! – and indicated that he should sit down.

"It was just a joke, OK, Jules?" she said, and wondered why Julian had turned a bright shade of red. Had he really been chatting up the new girl by the bar? And if he had been, why hadn't she been overly concerned about it? Indeed, she had been much more interested in Emma's friendly gossip about Vikram and the news of his new job.

Vikram, as though instinctively aware of some sort of mild tension between his two friends, said: "Linsey's a nice enough girl, isn't she, Jules? It was really kind of her to mention that job at Blades."

Julian nodded distractedly and then, when Emma and Vikram had got down to the much more serious business of demolishing Slinky Jo's cakes, he turned to his girlfriend, a serious look in his eyes.

"You do believe me when I say I wasn't coming on to her, don't you, Jackie?" he asked anxiously. "You know I'd never do anything to hurt you. I do love you so much..."

Jackie kissed him on the cheek. "Of course I believe you, Julian," she said. "And I love you so much too..."

But as she sipped at her double espresso, Jackie wondered if either of them was telling the truth.

2

Just as Emma had predicted, Vikram got the job at Blades ice-skating rink, and Miss Crabtree, the cranky middle-aged former skater who ran the place told him he could start on Monday. When he had asked her, rather sheepishly, whether he could let his friends come and use the ice rink for half-price, she had shaken her head firmly.

"Sorry, Miss Crabtree," Vikram said, and hung his head in embarrassment. "I guess it was a pretty cheeky thing to ask, especially as I haven't even started working here yet."

Miss Crabtree beamed a smile that none of her other colleagues would have dreamt her capable of, and said: "Nonsense, Vikram, they must come in for free. I'm sure a young man like yourself will only have upstanding and polite friends – unlike many of the hooligans we attract here nowadays. Call it my welcoming gift to you!"

Vikram couldn't believe his luck, and smiled at Miss Crabtree. The crusty old director of the rink felt her knees turn to jelly. "You really mean it?" he asked incredulously. He stood up to shake the woman's hand gratefully. "Hey, that's great. Thanks very much, Miss Crabtree."

"Think nothing of it, Vikram," Miss Crabtree said, and looked admiringly at the young man before her: if only she were thirty years younger! And he was so polite too, so different to the other young men of his age. If Emma had been eavesdropping on the conversation, she would by now have turned to Jackie and declared that Miss Crabtree had been "well and truly hooked".

Miss Crabtree released her hand from Vikram's, and showed him to the office door. As she opened it, a wave of cold air from the ice hit them, and they could hear the delighted shouts of the Saturday afternoon skaters, as their cries echoed in the huge hall.

"And of course, you have free use of the ice whenever you're not working," she said. "Apart from mornings of course, when lessons are being held."

"That's really sweet of you, Miss Crabtree," Vikram said. "But I don't skate. Every other sport going maybe, but not ice-skating."

"Then you must learn!" she decided. "We should fix you up with one of our instructors – maybe a pretty young girl?" she added with a twinkle in her eyes.

Vikram laughed. "I'm sure she'd find me incredibly clumsy," he said, self-deprecatingly. "I've got two left feet!"

"Well, the offer's still open," she said as she waved him goodbye. "And anything you want,

Vikram, just let me know, and I'm sure I'll be able to help. And Vikram, it's Betty – not Miss Crabtree – is that clear?"

Vikram chuckled. "Sure, Miss – I mean, Betty!"

"See? What did I tell you?" Emma said smugly, as she, Vikram and Jackie finished off the last of their noodles in the trendy Japanese sushi bar where they were meeting to celebrate Vikram's job. "Putty in your hands!"

Vikram laughed, and wiped his mouth with a paper napkin: there was a slice of green pepper on his lower lip, Jackie noticed. It made him look cute, like a little boy.

"Don't ask me what I did," he said. "It's not as if I have any experience! Apart from A-level maths of course – I guess that'll be helpful when I come to cash up in the evenings."

Emma shook her head, and placed a hand on Vikram's. "Vik, people like you don't need any experience," she said.

"I don't know what you mean," he replied, and meant it. "But then I guess I've always been lucky."

Lucky where women are concerned, Emma thought. *They all fall over themselves to be as nice to you as possible!*

"Anyway, enough talking about me and my new job," Vikram said, and turned to Jackie, who was idly prodding the last of her noodles with her chopsticks. "You've been quiet all evening. How are you feeling?"

"What?" Jackie looked up, suddenly aware that

Vikram was addressing her. She had been distracted, far away from the conversation.

"Are you OK?" he asked, and looked at her with those dark and soulful eyes of his. They were moist and fathomless, yet Jackie could see in them the genuine concern Vikram had for her. He had always looked out for her, even when they had been little kids; somehow she didn't know what she'd do without Vikram around the place. And yet he never dominated her like Julian, he always listened to her opinions. When Julian was taking her out for a meal, she sometimes felt like little more than an adjunct to his social life, almost a pretty accessory, a possession. With Vikram, she felt an equal, a friend.

"You've been looking like this all night," Emma said, and pulled a long face, which made even Jackie laugh.

"I'm fine," she said, and wasn't sure whether she was telling the truth or not. "I've just been thinking."

"About what?" Vikram asked.

Jackie shrugged. "Just things, that's all."

"About all the hunky ice-skaters who are going to take us for a spin around the ice starting next Monday," Emma decided gleefully.

Jackie giggled. "Don't you ever think of anything but boys, Em?" she asked, with a touch of mock-disapproval in her voice.

"Nope," Emma said, and then frowned: "Trouble is, all the boys are usually thinking of Sharon Stone or Winona Ryder and never little old me..."

Emma's joke defused what could have been a

potentially awkward situation, and Jackie finished her meal, rounding it off with a small glass of sake, the Japanese rice wine. Emma loved it but she found it a little too strong for her taste. Vikram was drinking water, as apart from the occasional can of cider he didn't drink at all. Jackie lowered her glass and smiled at Vikram.

"And thanks for inviting me out tonight to celebrate, Vik," she said. "It was so considerate and much better than staying in by myself and watching Saturday night telly."

Vikram smiled and told her not to mention it. "That's what friends are for," he said. "Emma told me how much you were looking forward to going out with Jules tonight – it's the least I could do." He caught the eye of the Japanese waitress by the cashdesk and she came over with the bill.

"Let me pick up the tab, Vik, by way of a thank-you," Jackie offered, and reached for her purse, but Vikram shook his head.

"I can't let you pay for it all!" she protested. That was exactly what Julian would do, she realized, but Vikram shook his head.

"What do you think I am? Made of money?" he asked, pretending to be outraged at the very thought. "We split it three ways."

"OK," agreed Emma. "A third each?"

Vikram turned to her, in wide-eyed horror. "You think I'm crazy, Emma Carter?" he gasped. "You and Jackie had much more than me: the sake for one thing! And you had the –" he snatched at the menu, and tried to pronounce the unfamiliar words – "the hamaguri ushiojiru!"

"The what?"

"The clam soup," Vikram explained. "At least I think that's what it is..."

"I did?" Emma asked.

"No, I did," Jackie butted in, and took the bill from Vikram, and a pen from out of her pocket. "Now let's make a list of what each of us had, OK? Vik, you had the seaweed, right?"

"Sure," he said, and, as Jackie scribbled the price down, added mischievously, "but you and Emma nicked half of mine so you two should go quarters on it!"

"But you tried one of my rice balls," Emma pointed out to him.

"Only one," Vikram said, but Emma wasn't to be swayed.

"I only had six," she said, and quoted a sixth of the price for a serving of rice balls.

"This is getting confusing," Jackie despaired, and for a second longed for the simpler times when Julian would pick up the entire tab.

"No, this is getting ridiculous," Emma corrected her, and laughed. She turned to Jackie and grinned: "It's surprising how much of a male chauvinist pig our Vik can be when he's talking about football; but when it comes to paying for the meal then he's all for equal rights!"

"You two girls have reformed my outmoded and traditionalist outlook on life," he claimed solemnly, with a hand over his heart.

"Got you worried about your bank balance is more like it," Jackie said.

"That as well," Vikram admitted. "We're all as

poor as each other: we haven't got super-rich daddies like Jules, you know! We're all equals."

Jackie agreed. "I could still have paid," she said, when the waitress had collected their bill, and a mixed array of crumpled fivers, fifty-pence and five-pence pieces. "After all, I was going to buy for Julian tonight."

"No way," Vikram said. "I don't like to be dependent on anyone. Equals, that's all that matters."

"I know what you mean," Jackie said, half to herself.

Before either Vikram or Emma could ask her what she meant, they spotted Linsey, the girl they had seen earlier at Slinky Jo's, on her way up to their table. She had just arrived with a group of people, both boys and girls, each and every one of them stunningly good-looking and insufferably trendy, and they were being shown to their table by a waitress.

"Fancy meeting you here!" she said, and when Vikram had introduced them gave Jackie and Emma each a brief polite nod, before turning all her considerable attention on Vikram. She was wearing a loud Versace blouse (which must have cost a small fortune, Jackie reckoned), and baggy leather trousers, and she looked a million dollars.

On second thoughts, Jackie seemed to say to Emma as they each exchanged a look, *make that two million dollars!*

"Er, hi, Linsey," Vikram smiled, and gave Jackie and Emma a *hey, what's a boy s'posed to do?* sort of look.

"And where's your other sexy friend, Vikram?" Linsey asked, her voice suggestive and hopeful. "That gorgeous blond guy, Julian?"

Vikram looked helplessly at Jackie, who smiled back at Linsey with all the sweetness and sincerity of a crocodile looking for its next meal.

"*My boyfriend* is at home, preparing for his future," she frostily informed Linsey. She couldn't believe the nerve of the sexy young newcomer! How dare she fancy *her* boyfriend!

Linsey, however, didn't miss a beat. "You must be soooo happy going out with him," she said, and looked Jackie up and down, as though sizing up the competition. "And surprised too. He's got to be the best thing that'll ever happen to you, Emma."

The implication was obvious, but Jackie kept her cool. *Maybe I'm the best thing that's ever happened to him,* she thought, but instead contented herself with correcting Linsey. "And my name's Jackie, not Emma." She nodded over to her friend. "This is Emma."

Linsey looked over at Emma, and then back at Jackie, and then at Emma again, as if she were comparing them. "Of course, how silly of me," she oozed. "How could I have got you mixed up? You're so different from each other. After all, Jackie, you're so slim..."

At Jackie's side Emma saw red, but Linsey had already turned away from them and was once again addressing Vikram, who hadn't seemed to have noticed that anything was amiss. It seemed that Linsey felt herself honour-bound to put down any females who might be an obstacle in her pursuit of the latest hunk, who in this case, and in the absence of Julian, seemed to be Vikram.

"So did you get the job?" she asked, and when Vikram nodded she let out a screech of delight, and hugged Vikram, planting an enormous kiss on his cheek, and then one full on the lips. Vikram sat back in his seat, totally disconcerted by Linsey's sudden display of affection.

Unwilling witnesses to Linsey's totally over-the-top behaviour, Jackie and Emma winced, but found they couldn't take their eyes off her. Much as they instinctively disliked her, each of them also felt a sneaking admiration. Certainly neither of them would ever have dared to try something like that on a boy they had only just started talking to that very afternoon!

"I knew you'd get it!" Linsey said categorically. "How could Betty refuse someone as good-looking as you? I hope we'll be seeing a lot more of each other now, Vikram."

"Well, sure, Linsey," Vikram said, trying to sound as noncommittal as possible. "But you know, I'm going to be busy, what with this new job, and I play a lot of sports and work out at the gym quite a bit too..."

Linsey's green eyes twinkled mischievously. "I bet you do!" she said, and reached out teasingly, to feel Vikram's biceps beneath the sleeves of his denim shirt. "I really like men with muscles who look after their bodies!"

Jackie and Emma exchanged another look: was this woman for real?

However, Vikram seemed slightly embarrassed

by all this teasing, and Linsey instantly picked up on it. She took her hand off his arm, as if it had just turned red-hot.

"But we will be seeing each other a lot more," she said, her voice suddenly less effusive than it had been only a second ago. "How do you think I heard of the job in the first place? I work there occasionally and Betty Crabtree, who runs Blades, is my aunt –"

Emma looked meaningfully at Jackie. She had described Betty Crabtree as an old dragon: it seemed that it ran in the family!

"– and I practise my ice-skating there every day," Linsey continued, and preened herself in front of them all, showing her firm and slim figure to its very best advantage. "I do think it's sooooo important for a girl to stay in shape these days – don't you? Unlike some people."

This last remark was addressed not at Vikram or even Jackie, but at the ever weight-conscious Emma. Somehow Linsey had zeroed in on the one thing guaranteed to upset Emma, who glared daggers at her. Linsey just smiled sweetly and returned to Vikram.

"Look, Vikram, my friends are over there," she said and waved at the group of nine or ten. "You must come over and meet them. I'm sure these two girls won't miss you for a while..."

Linsey wouldn't take no for an answer and hustled Vikram out of his chair. She started to lead him over to the table, when Emma, who had been quietly fuming to herself over Linsey's treatment of her, said: "It's OK, Vik, don't worry about us..."

"Hey, I'm sorry, Em," he said genuinely. "I'll just say hello to Linsey's friends and then I'll be straight back."

"That's right, Vik," Linsey said, and Jackie noticed that she had instantly picked up on their use of Vikram's nickname, and had adopted it herself.

"Of course you have set the VCR, haven't you?" Emma said casually, and Jackie stared at her: what was Emma talking about?

"The VCR?" Vikram's face went pale; this wouldn't be the first time that he had forgotten to set the video recorder to tape something off the television.

"Sky Sports," she said, and told him that the satellite channel was showing a three-hour special tribute to a famous footballing legend and one of Vikram's all-time heroes.

"But I didn't know..." said Vikram, who always made a point of circling in red in the *Radio Times* whatever sports programmes were being shown on satellite and cable.

"Change of schedule," was Emma's pat reply.

"Vik, forget about it," Linsey urged, and started to pull him towards her table. "It's only a silly little man kicking a football around."

"I can't miss this, Linsey!" he said. "He was the greatest striker of his generation!"

Linsey wasn't prepared to take no for an answer. "So get your parents to tape it."

"No can do," said Jackie, who had caught on to Emma's ruse and was enjoying the look of indignation on Linsey's face. "They've got two late-night shops to run. They won't be home till late."

"For goodness' sake," said Linsey, growing irritated now. "It's only a game of football after all!"

It was the wrong thing to say to Vikram. He released himself from Linsey's hold and looked at his watch: if he hurried he might just make it home in time.

"Look, Linsey, it's been really nice seeing you again," he said, making his exit. "And I'll look forward to seeing you on Monday at the rink."

"But..."

Vikram turned to Jackie and Emma and gave them each a farewell kiss on the cheek. "Thanks for reminding me, girls – you're real mates," he said gratefully, and not without some relief at being rescued from the clutches of the irrepressible Linsey. "I'll see you soon, OK?"

And with that Vikram grabbed the leather jacket he had thrown over the back of his chair, and was out of the restaurant, leaving a fuming Linsey staring angrily at Jackie and Emma.

"You know what boys of that age are like," Jackie said in a sarcastic tone of voice.

"Sports mad," Emma agreed. "No time for anything else – especially not girlfriends..."

Linsey glared at them and then, without saying a word stalked back to her own table.

"Em, you were marvellous!" Jackie congratulated her friend.

"At least it got her off Vik's back," Emma said. "She'd have made mincemeat out of him!"

"Lucky for him that he'd forgotten about that sports programme," Jackie said.

"That's hardly surprising as there isn't going to be a programme for him to tape when he gets back home!" Emma revealed, and giggled. "I made it all up to save our Vik from a fate worse than death!"

"He'll kill you when he finds out, you know," Jackie laughed.

"Either that or thank me for rescuing him from the clutches of our Black Widow Spider over there!"

"Did you see the way she treated him?" Jackie said distastefully. "Like he was a piece of meat, just another notch for her scorecard."

"He is an exceptionally good-looking guy, you know," Emma reminded her.

"Yeah, you said," Jackie said wistfully. "I guess he is..."

"Well, you hadn't noticed until I told you so this afternoon," Emma pointed out.

"He's never had a real girlfriend, has he?" Jackie continued. "Why do you suppose that is?"

Emma shrugged. "We've never discussed it," she said. "I suppose he's just been so busy, what with working hard for his A-levels, and all the sports he does. Some boys are like that – they much prefer to hang out with the rest of the other lads – more's the pity."

"But he must know just how attractive he is to the girls," Jackie said.

"He's like lots of good-looking people," Emma said. "They've no idea of how attractive they are, or the effect they have on others..."

"Unlike some people," Jackie said, and looked

over to the table where Linsey and her friends were ordering several bottles of sake. "What gives her the right to barge in here and think she can get any boy she wants?"

Emma looked curiously at her old friend. "Why are you so uptight about it, Jackie?" she asked. "It's not as if Vik's your boyfriend or anything. And I didn't see you getting so upset when she was talking to Julian in Slinky Jo's this afternoon, or when she mentioned just now how sexy she found Jules..."

"Don't mind me," Jackie said off-handedly. "I've probably just had too much sake..."

"Jackie, before Linsey burst in, you were agreeing with Vikram, saying that you didn't like being dependent on anyone," Emma said, choosing her words carefully. "Were you talking about Julian?"

Jackie eyed her friend, and then smiled. "I guess you've known me too well and for too long," she said.

"That's right," Emma said. "You, me and Vik have lived in the same neighbourhood since we were all little kids. And besides I read lots of problem pages!"

"It's not a problem," Jackie said automatically, and then sighed. "It's just that Jules does so much for me, sending me little presents, making sure I'm all right—"

"—And standing you up tonight!" Emma chipped in.

"But he gave me that cassette to make up for it. And no doubt I'll get yet another present tomorrow just to prove how sorry he is," Jackie said.

"He's a sweet guy," Emma remarked.

"But he never lets me do my own thing," Jackie said. "He's always there for me when I need him. But when does he ever need me? When does he ever let me do something for him? Sometimes it's like he's smothering me... And just when I get the nerve to..." She paused.

"To do what, Jackie?" Emma asked softly.

Jackie shook her head. "It doesn't matter, Em," she claimed, and looked over at Linsey's table, no longer bothering to hide the jealousy in her eyes. She turned back to Emma and attempted a brave smile.

"C'mon, Em, let's go home," she said brightly. "And on the way we can call in at Vikram's to apologize for sending him home early!"

"Sure," said Emma, and followed Jackie out of the sushi bar. As she did so, she wondered just what was going on in Jackie's mind. She remembered the conversation Jackie and Julian had had in Slinky Jo's, and all the presents that Julian had recently been giving Jackie.

Could it be that he was trying to ease a guilty conscience, Emma wondered. And then she recalled Jackie's surprise when she had pointed out just how good-looking Vikram was; and how annoyed she had been at Linsey's intrusion tonight. Could it be that Jackie was actually jealous? And what was it that Jackie had found the nerve to do, and wouldn't tell Emma?

Emma Carter, you have been reading too many trashy romances! she scolded herself, as she and Jackie hailed a taxi to take them home. *You're putting two and two together and coming up with five!*

But Emma had never been more wrong in her life, for she and Jackie were just about to discover that two and two most definitely do come to four.

3

"'Gorgeous blond guy'?" asked Julian in disbelief the following morning, as he and Vikram left the changing rooms of the local leisure centre.

"That's what she called you," Vikram said. "Seemed like she was really disappointed when you weren't at the sushi bar last night."

"Yeah, well, I had to see this friend of my dad's," Julian said off-handedly.

"Fair enough. What did he say? Give you any advice on applying for medical school?" Vikram asked, as they passed an exceptionally pretty young red-head on the stairs, who was dressed in a tight all-in-one Lycra outfit.

"Sorry?" Julian asked, and tore his eyes away from the girl. Vikram gave him a knowing smile. "What did you say, mate?"

"I asked if your dad's friend had given you any good tips on getting into medical school," Vikram repeated patiently.

"Ah that ... yes..." Julian coloured. "Well ... er ... actually he had to cry off at the last moment," he revealed. "Apparently there was some emergency at the hospital and he had to stay in overnight."

"That's a shame," Vikram said, and then a sudden thought struck him. "So why didn't you come out with us? You knew Emma and I had planned to take Jackie out 'cause you were tied up. You could have come along with us. Or gone out with Jackie to that country pub like she'd planned."

Julian stared straight ahead, desperately trying to avoid Vikram's eyes. "I ... I didn't feel like it, that's all," he said rather lamely. "I suppose I just fancied a quiet night in..."

Vikram reached out for Julian's arm and stopped him, making him turn around to look at him. "Jackie was so upset that you couldn't make it last night," he reminded his mate. "She was really looking forward to taking you out for dinner."

"She needn't do that," Julian said, and a tiny nervous tic appeared at the corner of his mouth. "I can easily afford to take both of us out."

"She wanted to do it herself," Vikram insisted. "And if you were just too tired to go out at least you could have rung her to apologize..."

"I ... I know..." Julian said, and then added after a long pause: "Look, Vik, perhaps I just wanted a night in by myself for a change..."

Vikram shrugged. "Sure. No problem." He still hadn't let go of Julian's arm. "Jules, are you sure that you were supposed to meet this friend of your dad's last night?"

Julian flushed even redder. "That's what I said, wasn't it?" he demanded angrily. "Hey, are you accusing me of lying? Of fooling around behind Jackie's back?"

"Forget it, Jules," Vikram said, and released Julian's arm. It was obvious from Julian's demeanour that he was telling the truth. "I mean, it's none of my business really. It's not like she's my girlfriend, is it?"

"Yeah, right on both counts, Vik," Julian said through gritted teeth. Vikram might be his best mate but that didn't mean that he had a right to snoop around into his private life. As it was, he had stayed in last night; but what did it have to do with Vik if he was two-timing Jackie or not? Not that he ever would, of course... "Keep your nose out of it, OK?"

"Just make sure that you don't hurt Jackie, that's all," Vikram warned.

There was a dangerous flash in Julian's eyes. "And what's it to you if I do?" he hissed.

"Look, she might be your girlfriend, but she's my friend," Vikram said, surprised at the force of Julian's anger – and, indeed, at his own. "Jackie and I go back a long way. We used to look out for each other, that's all."

The angry look in Julian's eyes passed, and he was his old self once again. "Of course she is," he said, and took a few deep breaths to control his voice. "I understand that."

"I just don't want to see her unhappy, that's all," said Vikram, still observing Julian through dark, suspicious eyes.

"Why would I want to hurt her?" Julian asked and there was a tremor in his voice which Vikram had never heard before. "She's my girlfriend. We've been going out for over two years. I love her. And she loves me."

Vikram smiled, and offered his hand to Julian. "OK, Jules, no questions asked," he said, his brief doubt past. "Friends?"

"Friends," said Julian, and shook Vikram's proffered hand. "But let's keep this one to ourselves, hey? I promise that I would never cheat on Jackie, but you know what she's like. If she finds out I stayed in last night she'll start thinking all the wrong things..."

Exactly the same sort of things I was thinking just now, Vikram realized, but nevertheless agreed to keep Julian's little secret. Maybe he was telling the truth and he just wanted a night in, although Vikram couldn't see why Julian would rather watch Saturday night telly than have an intimate dinner *à deux* with one of the most popular girls Vikram knew. And for free, as well! Vik knew that lots of his mates would have jumped at the opportunity to take Jackie out; some of them had even mentioned to Vikram how sexy they found her. That had puzzled Vikram: he couldn't really see it himself. As far as he was concerned, Jackie was just, well, Jackie – one of his very best friends.

Julian slapped Vikram on the back like one of the lads sharing a private joke with his best mate. "It's all for the best," he claimed. "You've got to handle women carefully, otherwise they go off at the deep end, get the wrong end of the stick, and then it's hell getting them sweet again."

Vikram smiled awkwardly. "Then I'll bow to your wealth of experience on that one, Jules!" he said light-heartedly.

Julian chuckled, like a man of the world, instead of a seventeen-year-old who had only ever had one girlfriend in his entire life. "You'll understand when you start dating the girls!" he reassured him.

"Not much chance of that at the moment," Vikram said, a touch of gloom entering the conversation.

Julian halted on the stairs again (taking the opportunity, this time, of briefly ogling a pretty blonde in a tracksuit who was passing them). "C'mon, Vik, they must be queuing up to go out with you," he said. "Only the other day Clare Bond told me how much she fancied you and asked me to fix her up with you for a foursome with me and Jackie."

"She did?" Vikram knew Clare very well – a pretty girl in a nice self-effacing way. He hadn't the slightest idea that she fancied him, even though they'd spent the past two years studying A-level maths together.

"That's right, Vik, you're a popular man in these parts!"

"Only not as popular as you are, it seems," Vikram said, and instantly regretted what he'd said. If Julian really was cheating on Jackie, as he suspected, then it was none of his business.

Or was it?

However, Julian chose not to pick up on the remark – *a guilty conscience or what?* Vikram wondered – and instead asked: "What did you mean? That there's not much chance of dating anyone at the moment?"

Vikram smiled stoically. "Mum and Dad," he explained. "You know how strict they are."

Julian nodded: he had met Mr and Mrs Pandy, Vikram's parents once before, when he was picking Vikram up to go to a party and they had looked disapprovingly at the six-pack of cider he had brought with him for he and Vikram to share. "I didn't think you let that sort of tradition bother you."

"I don't," Vikram admitted. "My parents might still be kinda traditional in some respects but I regard myself as much more English than Pakistani now. But they've picked out a girl they want me to marry."

"An arranged marriage?" Julian asked, and gave a low sympathetic whistle. "Are you going to go ahead with it?"

Vikram shook his head. "No way," he said.

"I heard that some of these marriages can work out," Julian said. "And they grow into love later."

"That's right," Vikram agreed. "But I want to love the person I marry before the wedding."

"So what's the problem?" Julian asked. "OK, you'll get some hassle from your parents, but everyone gets that for one reason or another whether they come from Bangalore or Birmingham!"

"The problem is that the girl they want me to marry – Lakshmi Patel – is the daughter of a friend of my dad's. She's a great girl by all accounts, and the Patels are a respected family."

"Lots of Indian and Pakistani guys refuse to marry the person their parents have chosen for them," Julian pointed out. "Tradition's all very fine, but times change. OK, you might upset your dad for a while, and this Patel guy might strike him off the Christmas card list for a couple of years –"

"We're Muslims," Vikram said with a smile. "We don't send Christmas cards..."

Julian chuckled. "That's never stopped you from going to all the Christmas parties, Vik," he said. "But seriously: they'll get over it. You've got to follow your own feelings in this world, do what you want to do –" he paused for a moment before adding, with a slight touch of regret in his voice – "as long as it doesn't hurt anyone else of course..."

"If it was just a matter of tradition it wouldn't be so difficult," Vikram said. "After all, I've been winding Dad up for years now breaking every tradition in the book. But there's an added complication."

"With you there always is, big buddy," Julian laughed and slapped him amiably on the back.

"Mr Patel is a businessman and he's not short of cash," Vikram revealed. "He's suggested that he might want to invest in a major way in my dad's two stores..."

"Aha," said Julian. "I see the problem. You ditch this Lakshmi girl, and it's bye-bye to your dad's plans to expand his business?"

"Something like that, yes," said Vikram.

"And have you seen this girl yet?" asked Julian.

"Only photos. Her dad's bringing her over to England quite soon to meet my parents and me."

"And?"

"She's pretty – very pretty," Vikram said. "In any other circumstances I'd probably ask her out on a date myself! If it didn't get in the way of football practice, of course."

"But you wouldn't want to marry her?"

"That's right. Not now, at any rate."

Julian frowned. "Not now? What d'you mean?"

Vikram smiled. "Let's leave it, shall we?" he suggested as they finally reached the leisure centre's café area, where Jackie and Emma were waiting for them. "I've said more than I should have done anyway. You don't bring up the subject of Lakshmi again, and I won't mention to Jackie that you stayed in last night. Is that a deal?"

"It's a deal, Vik," Julian said, and walked up and kissed Jackie.

"And how was your game of squash?" Jackie asked.

"I trashed him," Vikram cut in. "As usual!"

"Hard luck," Jackie said. "And how was last night, Jules?"

"Huh?"

"Your dad's friend, remember?" Jackie said, not noticing the look of complicity which passed between the two boys.

"Oh, that was fine, he told me some really useful things," Julian lied. "Let's all have a coffee and then, as the loser, I guess it's my turn to buy us all Sunday lunch!"

"Jules, you shouldn't," Jackie protested, even though Emma hushed her – a free slap-up meal sounded like a pretty good idea to her!

"I insist!" said Julian. "It's the least I can do!"

Definitely a guilty conscience, thought Vikram, as he followed the others to the serving hatch to collect their cups of instant.

And his heart went out to Jackie.

He wasn't quite sure why.

4

Blades Ice-Skating Rink was one of the oldest ice-skating rinks in the country and it showed. Around the oval-shaped ice-rink rose fluted columns which betrayed its previous existence as an old-time music hall; and the domed roof from which paste-glass chandeliers had once hung, now made a perfect echo chamber, amplifying the screams of delight as ice-skaters whizzed round the ice, or their squeals of surprise as the less experienced of them fell flat on their backs.

Beyond the padded crash barriers, there were rows of uncomfortable-looking seats, which were used by spectators. Twice a year Betty Crabtree organized an ice gala, and printed on the tickets there was always an encouragement to the members of the audience to bring their own cushions to sit on. Bruised knees and elbows were hazards of ice-skating which even the most professional ice-skaters couldn't avoid; but bruised backsides were another matter entirely!

At one end of the oval rink there was an organ which, like the elaborate painted designs and fretwork on the columns, had obviously seen better days. It was rarely played now and the ice-skaters moved around the rink to bland and repetitive muzak piped over the PA system, or to the chart sounds of the local independent radio station.

Sitting by the organ, in front of a control board, and watching the action on the ice, was a weasly looking man; obviously a former ice-skater, who, like the rest of the building, was dreaming of finer and younger days.

The only concession to modernity was a series of frescoes lining the back of one of the walls, paintings of famous British ice-skaters such as Torvill and Dean, and Karen Slater and Nicky Campbell; or at least that's what Betty Crabtree told all her customers, although, as Emma had once said, "If that's supposed to be Torvill and Dean, then I'm Naomi Campbell!"

Up a small flight of steps, opposite the neglected organ and overlooking the rink, was Blades' café-cum-bar, which served a selection of sandwiches and soft drinks, and where the wall-length window offered diners the best view of the ice-skaters below. It was here that Vikram was working, and as Jackie, Emma and Julian walked into the rink early on Monday afternoon they waved up at him. He smiled and waved back, before returning to his work behind the counter.

Jackie and Emma owned their own skates, and, as they sat down on a pair of slatted wooden benches to tighten up the laces on their boots, Julian went off to the rink's office to hire a pair. Jackie and Emma used the opportunity to eye up the talent on the rink.

A couple of Italian guys – the same two Jackie had spotted in the high street on Saturday – were racing each other around the edge of the rink. They were alone, so it seemed that their flirting with the two girls hadn't gone as successfully as Jackie had predicted.

In the centre of the rink, away from the skating *hoi polloi*, a few small girls, dressed in skating tutus (unlike everyone else who was wearing either sensible tracksuits or jeans and baggy T-shirts), were practising their movements. Accompanying them on the ice were their individual ice-skating teachers, casually-dressed men and women only a few years older than Jackie and Emma. They were whispering words of encouragement to their charges, and giving them a brief round of applause every time they executed a perfect double or triple axel. Watching from the sidelines were the little girls' proud mothers, swapping gossip with the other mothers, and saying just how good their own daughter was. Apart from them there were only about another dozen or so people on the ice, most of them couples.

"So where are all the hunks you said were going to be here, Em?" Jackie asked, as she walked unsteadily on her skates across the rubber-matted floor and to the edge of the ice, where she held on to the surrounding rail for support.

"They'll be here sooner or later," Emma said

confidently. "Anyway I'm the one who's supposed to be hunk-hunting, not you! You've got Julian, remember?"

"Of course," said Jackie. She put a tentative foot on the ice. Her feet started to move from under her, and she grabbed a tighter hold of the rail. She looked worriedly at Emma. "Em, do you think this is such a good idea after all? It's been almost eighteen months since I was last ice-skating."

Emma laughed. "It's exactly like riding a bike," she insisted. "You never forget. You just have to get your old confidence back, that's all!"

Then she stepped gingerly on to the ice, positioned her feet into the form of a "T", and pushed off, gliding around the ice with supreme ease, as though she had been born on it and had never done anything else. Jackie watched approvingly: Emma might at times be unsure of herself, but on the ice she moved with confidence and grace. Deciding that if she was going to fall and make a total fool of herself, it might as well be sooner rather than later, Jackie followed Emma on to the main body of the ice.

Contrary to her expectations, she didn't fall, but slid smoothly off after Emma, enjoying the feel of the crisp cold "breeze" as she raced around the ice. The feeling of almost effortless motion invigorated her, making whatever troubles she had seem meaningless, as she remembered in an instant all she thought she'd forgotten. She wondered why she'd ever stopped ice-skating in the first place: surely this sense of freedom and ease was one of the most wonderful feelings in the world! After a few circuits of the ice she scrunched to a halt by Emma, her cheeks ruddy and healthy with the exercise.

"Wasn't that great?" she said, and then asked Emma why she had stopped. She looked in the direction Emma's finger was pointing.

"Will you look at that!" Emma said. "It seems that my theory about hunks was right after all!"

Skating slowly towards them across the ice was a tall blond-haired guy a couple of years older than them. Even at this distance they could see that he had piercing blue eyes, the clear smooth complexion of a model ("We're talking *GQ* here, Jackie," Emma said confidently), and the sort of body that only years in the gym could have produced.

Emma would have gone even further and described him as "Sex On Ice", if Jackie hadn't got in first.

"Jackie! I'm surprised at you!" Emma said admiringly.

"Just don't tell Jules!" Jackie giggled, and glanced behind her. Julian was still putting on his skates and hadn't noticed them yet. "But he is a bit of all right!"

The handsome and sexy newcomer glided to a halt in front of them, stopping with the sort of smooth ease that Jackie knew she'd never be able to manage, even with years of practice. Without knowing why, Jackie glanced guiltily up at the café: Vikram was serving behind the counter and, like Julian, was too busy to notice them.

The blond boy smiled at each of them in turn, dazzling them with his brilliantly white smile.

"Hi," he said. His voice was deep and friendly; he sounded Scandinavian, although there was also the faint trace of an American accent in his voice. He'd probably spent some time in the States where he had perfected his English, Emma guessed, and remembered just how skating-mad some of her American friends were.

"Hi," said Jackie. Emma merely nodded; confronted with what she'd describe as "drop-dead gorgeousity", for once she was lost for words. That had always been her trouble: she'd rehearsed over and over in her head all the best chat-up lines, but when it came to trying them out on a real-live hunk, she went all to pieces.

"I was watching you out there on the ice," he said. "You were both very good."

"Rubbish," said Jackie.

"You really think so?" asked Emma.

"Seriously," he said, and smiled at her again, with a smile that could make even the ice melt. "And I should know. My name's Adam. I'm one of the skating instructors here."

Jackie smiled and introduced Emma and herself; Adam shook them both by the hand.

"I haven't seen either of you here before," he said.

"That's right," said Jackie. "It's been eighteen months or so since I was last on the ice."

"You wouldn't know it," Adam chuckled. "You skate like a real pro!"

"Flattery will get you nowhere," Jackie said, and found herself blushing. She looked up at the café: she could see Vikram serving one of the skating mothers who was treating her little girl to a strawberry milkshake and telling Vikram what a star her daughter was.

"And you're really good as well," Adam said, and turned to Emma. Emma blushed even redder than Jackie: was this hunk actually *talking* to her? Did her existence even matter to him?

"Er ... thanks," muttered Emma, and wished the Earth would open up and swallow her whole.

Adam was going to say something else to Emma, when they all became aware of someone skating up behind them. Jackie turned, to see Julian approaching. He had only been out ice-skating once or twice before and he was still wobbly on his feet. His brow was furrowed with concentration as he slipped up to the three of them: Jackie held her hand out to him to help him stop, a pretty important movement on the ice which Julian still hadn't quite got the hang of.

Jackie introduced Julian to Adam and the two boys exchanged a polite and cursory nod of greeting. As she did so, the music being blasted through the PA system changed from the usual bland muzak to this year's Number One hit from last year's Hot Teen Idol from Down Under. The weasly guy at the microphone announced that it was time for "pairs" skating, and everyone not with a partner should leave the ice.

Julian groaned. "Can't we sit this one out?" he begged.

"Don't be stupid, Jules," Jackie said. "You've only just got out on the ice!"

"Yes," said Adam. "It'll be fun. We'll make up a

foursome." As Jackie was obviously Julian's girlfriend he looked over at Emma.

Emma, however, slid to Julian's side and took his arm. "C'mon, I'll be gentle with you!" she promised, and dragged him away from the others. As she did so she mentally kicked herself for shyly refusing Adam's offer of a pair-dance: it looked like she was her own worst enemy! Why was it that she always steered clear of boys she found attractive? Was it because she was scared of being rejected, afraid that her more attractive and experienced friends might think she was trying for someone way out of her league?

Adam sighed and gave Jackie a sheepish look. "Well, it looks like you and me, doesn't it?" he said and winked encouragingly at her.

"So it does..." Jackie said, and taking hold of Adam's hand, she allowed him to lead her on to the ice.

It felt good holding Adam's hand as they circled the ice, their fingers intertwined, and Jackie was aware of several girls watching from the side and throwing envious looks in her direction. As she gained confidence on the ice, so Adam increased his speed, and he encircled her waist with a strong muscular arm. She glanced behind her at Julian and Emma, laughing and joking as they sped around the ice. Jackie felt slightly put out at the fact that Julian was grinning, seemingly unconcerned that his girlfriend was skating with the most gorgeous and desirable male on the ice, but when she looked up into Adam's face his smile made her beam even more. The light seemed to reflect off the ice and back into his blue eyes, making them sparkle and glitter like twin sapphires.

Jackie felt Adam's hand softly massage her lower back as he guided her around the ice, and she experienced a thrill of delight as she realized that here she was, skating with the sexiest and hunkiest boy on the ice.

Soon Jackie had forgotten all about Julian and Emma who had now caught up with them and were skating somewhere up ahead: all that seemed to matter was her and Adam, moving as one in a perfect display of ice-dancing.

"Not bad – for amateurs!"

"Sorry?"

At the cash register in the café, Vikram turned around, after handing his latest customer her change. Linsey was standing before him, dressed, as usual in a stylish designer top and jeans.

"Your friends down there on the ice," Linsey said, and nodded over to the large spectators' window. "They're not bad."

Vikram tried to look, but couldn't see from where he was standing. He beckoned to one of his colleagues – a sixteen-year-old girl who, in the two hours she had been working with Vikram had decided that she was totally, a hundred and one per cent, and irretrievably, in love with him.

"Yes, Vikram?" she breathed.

"Do us a favour and look after the till for a minute, will you?" Vikram asked. "I want to see Jackie and Emma do their stuff."

"Sure, Vikram," the lovestruck schoolkid said, and took his place at the till.

Linsey took Vikram's arm and led him to the window. "How was your football programme on TV the other night?" she asked, her voice full of friendly interest.

"What?" he said and then remembered: "Oh, that! Emma and Jackie got the wrong day."

"Did they now?" Linsey asked, and her voice suddenly turned as frosty as the ice below on the rink.

Vikram, however, didn't detect the change in Linsey's attitude, and instead looked down on to the ice. "She's great, isn't she?" he said admiringly, a strange note of fondness in his voice. "I mean, they both are... I wish I could skate like that..."

"I could teach you," Linsey said. "I'm sure I could teach you lots of things." She put a hand on Vikram's arm. He shook his head.

"I'd probably make an idiot of myself and fall flat on my face the minute I got on the ice," he said, self-deprecatingly.

"You should have confidence in your own abilities," Linsey said, looking hard at Vikram's profile – the collar-length hair, the full lips, and the firm chin. Vikram, however, didn't return her look, but continued to gaze out of the window.

"That's what I'm always telling Jackie," Vikram chuckled. "Who's that guy she's skating with?"

Linsey stopped considering Vikram's profile, and turned to look at the skaters. As Vikram knew Julian, it was obvious he was talking about Adam. An evil look came into her eyes.

"That's the new ice-skating instructor," she said, remembering having seen him the other day when Betty Crabtree was showing him around the rink. "I hear he's a bit of a charmer – a real ladies' man. Has all the skating mothers hopelessly in love with him: you should watch out for your two friends down there!"

Linsey frowned when she saw the flash of regret in Vikram's fathomless dark eyes; it disturbed her. "It's odd, isn't it," she continued, "dancing with the hunky skating teacher instead of her boyfriend..."

"What are you trying to imply?" Vikram asked her, a strange edge in his voice, as he protested his friend's faithfulness to Julian. There was also something else there too, Linsey realized, a wistfulness, almost hope. Of a disappointed man clutching desperately at straws.

Linsey smiled. "I was speaking out of turn and I'm sorry," she lied. "I'm sure she and her boyfriend are the greatest couple since Romeo and Juliet! Neither of them would dream of flirting with or looking at someone else..."

"You've got that right," Vikram said, and there was now no mistaking the melancholy in his voice. "Jackie and Julian are as close as close can be."

"Of course," said Linsey, although the way she said it clearly indicated that she didn't really mean it. "It was just that she and Adam looked so good together..."

5

"We were so good together," Adam said as pairs-skating ended and he and Jackie slid to a halt by the crash barriers. It was the sort of graceful stop that Jackie knew she could never achieve by herself; but with Adam everything seemed so natural, so effortless.

"Yes, we were," Jackie breathed, and looked up into his face. His cheeks were red, like hers, and there was a happy smile on his face. He was so handsome, Jackie decided, and she scarcely realized that he hadn't yet taken his arm from around her waist. "I've never found skating so easy before."

"That's because you had confidence in yourself," Adam said.

Confidence that you gave me, Jackie found herself thinking.

"I couldn't have done it without you, Adam," she said.

"Of course you could," Adam said, and finally

took his hand away from her waist. "You're good – very good –" Jackie started to protest, but Adam silenced her. "You know that Betty – Miss Crabtree – holds an ice-skating gala every Christmas here?"

"Of course I do," Jackie said. "It's her chance to show off her prize pupils to the town, and hopefully get a few more charitable donations to keep the place going."

"That's right," said Adam. "With a couple of months' practice you could even take part in it yourself. You're a natural, Jackie. With extra training and some lessons, you could be very good indeed."

Jackie pooh-poohed the notion. "With you as my teacher, I suppose?" she scoffed. "Adam, I know how much ice-skating lessons cost by the quarter-hour! I've got better things to spend my money on!"

"Have it your own way," Adam laughed. "But Betty always makes sure that there are talent scouts at every one of her galas. You never know, someone might spot your potential..."

"Now I know that you're leading me on!" Jackie said, even though she still couldn't take her eyes away from Adam's handsome face. "I'm seventeen. If a talent scout is going to pick on anyone as a promising professional skater it's going to be one of those skating kids over there –" she nodded over at the young girls, who had returned to the ice, watched over, as usual, by their adoring mothers – "I'm far too old!"

"Whatever you say," said Adam, and pretended to sulk, making himself look even more endearing

– *if that's possible*, Jackie thought. "That is, if you really want to turn down my offer of the chance to astound the world – not to mention every major ice-skating hunk in the country –"

"I have a boyfriend," Jackie said. "I don't need to impress anyone else."

"Yes, I know," Adam said, and sulked. "That's really such a great pity..."

Jackie laughed. "Are you flirting with me?" she asked happily.

Adam nodded and gave her the sort of smile that any girl in the rink would have died for. "Maybe I am teasing you a little," he admitted. "Only don't tell your boyfriend: I'm sure he'd pick a fight with me..."

"No, he wouldn't," Jackie said. "Julian's not like that." Somehow she could never imagine Julian fighting over her; indeed at times he seemed to take her so much for granted that she wondered if he'd even notice if anyone was coming on to her!

Adam looked slyly at Jackie. "I'm holding some special classes on Wednesday evenings," he said. "I've still got a half-hour window free..."

Jackie paused for a moment, and looked at Julian and Emma who were approaching. Julian had promised to take her out on Wednesday to the movies. After that he'd suggested that they go on to a posh new bistro which had just opened up down the road from Slinky Jo's.

No doubt there he would treat her to a slap-up meal, insisting that she didn't spend a penny, and they would certainly have a great time. He'd choose the wine, usually a Californian rosé which she hated, but she didn't dare tell Jules that because they both knew that it was generally acknowledged to be the trendy drink of the moment.

Afterwards they might even go out to a club of Julian's choice (of course), where they would dance the night away, before Julian would order a mini-cab to take her home. It was a lifestyle which many girls would have killed for, and yet Jackie was finding it more and more oppressive. Sometimes, she felt, she would like to do something for herself, make her own decisions, rather than being constantly looked after by Julian.

"That's a wonderful idea, Adam," she heard herself saying. "Shall we start this Wednesday?"

Adam grinned. "Great!" he said, and greeted Julian and Emma who were skating up to them.

Jackie felt her heart sink. What had possessed her to agree to Adam's suggestion? And how was she going to break the news to Julian that their date for Wednesday was off? And why was she looking forward to her skating lesson with Adam with all her heart?

"You two had a good time?" Julian asked innocently, and Jackie nodded.

"Your girlfriend's a good skater," Adam said, and added: "She's agreed to come to my lesson on Wednesday evening..."

"Wednesday?" Julian asked, and Adam nodded, unsure of what all the fuss was about. Julian looked at Jackie. "I thought we had a date then...?"

Jackie sighed, and felt her face flush red with

embarrassment. "I know, Jules," she started, "but Adam says I've got lots of talent and this is a great opportunity and I'll make it up to you and..."

Julian's eyes narrowed. "I understand," he said emotionlessly, and looked from Jackie to Adam and then back to Jackie.

"It's not what you think," Jackie protested.

"Hey, if I've caused any sort of problem between you two..." Adam began.

Julian glowered at him. "There's no problem," he said, perhaps not as bitterly as Jackie might have expected. "Why shouldn't Jackie take skating lessons with you? After all, that's probably much more important than me taking her out for a meal and to a club..."

"Jules, please..." said Jackie, and considered cancelling her ice-skating lesson there and then.

No, why should I? she scolded herself. *It's about time that I did something I wanted to do! It's about time that I asserted some sort of independence and stopped being continually at Jules' beck and call!*

"I'm going off to change," Julian said, and started to move off the ice. He turned back to look at Jackie. "I suppose I'm still allowed to give you a lift home afterwards?"

Jackie sighed. "Of course," she said, and watched as Julian went off to the boys' changing room.

Adam shrugged. "I'm sorry if I've made things awkward," he said.

"It's not your fault, Adam," Jackie said. "It's Julian's. He always likes to have things his own way ... he gets really grumpy when people start thinking for themselves..."

Adam nodded, and said, in his Scandinavian-American accent, that he could "really relate to that", and then excused himself: he had a class in a few minutes with a seven-year-old girl who showed lots of promise, and could even become a professional skater with the right training.

After Adam had gone, Emma looked disapprovingly at her friend. "What do you think you're playing at, Jackie Taylor?" she asked. "Standing Jules up for someone you've only just met, even if he is so hot that I'm surprised the ice isn't melting?"

"Don't you start on me!" Jackie snapped, and then apologized. "OK, maybe I did get a little carried away then and didn't think things through. But I see Jules every day; why can't I just do something on my own for a change?"

"Jules loves you," Emma said softly. "He only wants what's best for you."

"I know," Jackie said. "But sometimes he smothers me with all his attention... And out there just now on the ice with Adam..."

"Yes?"

Jackie shrugged. "It just felt so natural, so free..." she said. "I've never felt that way with Julian..."

Emma smiled and shook her head. "Typical!" she said, and threw her hands up in the air in a gesture of mock despair. "I come to Blades to find a boyfriend, and who gets off with the hottest and most fanciable hunk on the ice but my best friend – who's already got a hunky boyfriend!"

"It's not like that, Emma," Jackie said, in a voice which carried very little conviction.

"Isn't it?" Emma asked. "I've seen you over the past few weeks. Looking at the other boys in Slinky Jo's. Staring into space when Jules has been talking to you. You're not getting tired of him, by any chance?"

"Tired of him? Of course not," she said, and averted her eyes from Emma.

She stared up at the café. Vikram was still there, watching her; Linsey was standing by his side, and Jackie felt a strange pang. She turned back to Emma.

"Julian is a lovely, sweet guy, and I'd never do anything to hurt him, you know that. I really like him a lot..."

Like him a lot, Emma nodded wisely to herself; only a few months ago Jackie was declaring her undying love for Julian. She was about to say a few further words when she felt something hit her in the back. One of the Italian boys who had been racing his friend around the ice, collided into her, pushing her forward. She bumped into Jackie and they both fell crashing to the floor.

"You idiot!" Jackie shouted from where she had fallen on the ice, in an undignified heap. "What the hell do you think you're playing at?"

The Italian guy shrugged his apologies, and said something along the lines that if they wanted to stand still on the ice gossiping like a pair of old fishwives, then they should expect to get knocked over. He was remonstrating wildly and from a distance it could have looked as if things were about to turn nasty. He started swearing at Jackie and Emma, when he felt two powerful hands grip his shoulders, and he was forced to turn around, almost losing his balance on the ice.

"Don't you think you'd better apologize properly to the lady, you creep?"

They all turned around to see Vikram; he had rushed down from the café at the first sign of trouble, and there was a dangerous look on his face.

"Hey, look, it was an accident," the boy said. "I couldn't help running into your girlfriend."

"She's not my girlfriend," came Vikram's answer, a little too quickly.

"Vikram, it's OK," Jackie said, who was still sitting on the ice, but Vikram would hear nothing of it. He grabbed the Italian by his T-shirt with one hand, and waved his fist in his face. Sure enough, faced with such a convincing argument, the Italian guy duly made his apologies to Jackie, and Vikram released him.

"Vikram, there was no need to do that," Jackie said, after the Italian boy had left, and Vikram leant over to help her to her feet again. Both she and Emma had been taken aback by his sudden aggression: usually the only thing that got Vikram worked up was the latest Test Match results, or the woeful performance of his favourite football team.

"He was causing you grief," Vikram said. "I just didn't want to see you hurt, that's all... You know I've always been here for you whenever you needed me..."

His strong firm hands took hold of Jackie's arms and he pulled her gently to her feet. Jackie's feet slipped on the ice, and she fell against Vikram. For a second she remained like that, the full length of her body pressed against Vikram's. She felt his heart beating against her chest, felt his strong hands on her back; she looked up into his face, seeing in his dark eyes something she had never seen before.

Then the moment passed, and Vikram let go of her. They smiled shyly at each other, and exchanged an awkward look.

"You OK now?" Vikram asked.

"Of course," Jackie said, formally, denying the wild, confusing emotions she was feeling within herself, or the outrageous thoughts that were running madly inside her head: *This is crazy! Do you realize what you're thinking of? This isn't supposed to happen!*

"Would a certain hunky gentleman remember his good manners and help a deeply distressed damsel up off the floor?"

Vikram and Jackie both looked down at Emma who was still sitting on the ice, making a great play of tapping her fingers impatiently, and wearing an enormous frown. The tension broken, Jackie and Vikram burst out laughing, and Vikram helped Emma up.

"Thank you," Emma said frostily to her friend, and Vikram affected an extravagant courtly bow, like a gallant seventeenth-century cavalier. As he did so, his feet slipped on the ice, and, after a few moments' un-cavalier-like wobbling, he lost his balance and tumbled to the ground with a – for Emma – delightfully loud *thunk*! Jackie and Emma creased up with laughter.

"C'mon, girls, help me up!" Vikram pleaded.

"No way!" Emma said, and skated away from Vikram, who remained sitting in a cross-legged position as he watched his two friends glide away.

Or rather he watched Jackie glide away, and a troubled frown crossed his brow. Why had he been so anxious to rush down to help Jackie when he had seen her fall on the ice? After all, people fell down on the ice all the time at Blades, and suffered, at the most, a blow to their dignity. And he knew that Jackie was more than capable of shrugging off the unwanted advances of any oversexed Latino teenager.

Hey, she's my mate, of course, he reasoned to himself. *And that's what friends are for!*

But deep down Vikram knew that he wasn't fooling himself. Even though he lacked the courage to admit it, he knew what had passed between him and Jackie just a few moments ago on the ice. And he was just thankful that no one else had noticed it.

But Emma *had* noticed the look that Vikram and Jackie had exchanged. She was full of foreboding for her two friends, and was only grateful that Julian hadn't been there to see it too.

Someone else had, however. Up in the café, Linsey cursed under her breath, and vowed vengeance on Jackie.

6

"And you seriously expect me to believe that he's just your teacher?" Emma asked, as she watched Jackie get ready for her first ice-skating lesson in front of her bedroom mirror.

Jackie coloured, and applied a faint layer of pale-pink lipstick, which, along with the soft blusher on her cheeks, was something she normally never wore. "Of course," she said. "It's only your dirty mind that's reading things into it that aren't there!"

"Adam and Julian – two of the sexiest boys around, and both of them crazy for you!" Emma teased. Yet there was a longing in her voice that her cheery manner couldn't quite disguise. "And I bet Adam's giving you these lessons for free!"

"They're not crazy about me!" Jackie protested a little too earnestly. "Well, at least Adam isn't... And the lessons aren't free either. I landed myself a Saturday job down at the record store in town, so I'm paying for them myself." She looked at herself in the mirror, checking that her make-up was fine, and then asked casually: "Do you really think he is crazy about me? Adam, I mean..."

Emma shrugged. "Vikram thinks so," she said finally. "Not that he seemed particularly happy about it..."

"Vikram?" Jackie asked and then panicked. "What have you been telling Vik, Em? Oh my God, if he tells Jules..."

"Steady on," Emma said. "Vik won't say anything. All he said to me was that he'd seen the two of you out on the ice together, and that he thought that Adam really liked you. He was certainly paying you a lot of attention!"

"But Jules is still upset with me for not going out with him today," Jackie said. "Even though I let him take me out last night instead. Maybe I ought to ring Vik and get him to explain it all to Jules..."

Emma looked curiously at Jackie. "Ring Vik?" she repeated. "Don't you mean ring Jules?"

"Yes, of course I do," Jackie said, and stood up to go to the telephone which was on the landing, just outside her bedroom door.

"There's no point in phoning him," Emma advised. "It's Vik's day off so they've both gone out for the day – to a rugby match."

"God, how boring!" Jackie said, and relaxed again, now that the prospect of another awkward phone call with her boyfriend had been postponed. "I don't appreciate the attraction of football, but I can't even understand the rules of rugby!" She smoothed her hands over her trim figure, made more appealing by the tight T-shirt, and Lycra leggings she was wearing. "How do I look?"

"You look great," Emma said approvingly, even though she wondered why Jackie wasn't wearing her usual outfit of sloppy sweatshirt and jeans. She stood up and followed Jackie out of her bedroom and on to the landing.

"Jackie," she began, and her voice was suddenly serious. "I'm one of your best friends, and you know that I don't want to see you hurt..."

Jackie frowned, both uncomfortable and surprised at Emma's sombre manner and the direction in which the conversation had turned.

"I know that, Em..."

"But I'm also Jules' friend," Emma continued, "and I don't want to see him hurt either. You wouldn't cheat on him, would you?"

Jackie's face turned white – with rage? with indignation? with the awful knowledge that she had been found out? – and for a second Emma thought that Jackie was going to lash out at her, as she realized that she had hit a very sore point. Then the moment passed, and Jackie sighed and hugged herself, as if for comfort.

"I don't know, Em," she said finally, looking not at her friend, but at the ceiling, as though she was reluctant to look at Emma's face and the disapproving look she was sure she would find there. "Jules is one of the most wonderful guys in the world, and he always treats me like a queen. Especially recently, although heaven knows why. We have some wonderful times together. But when he's not there I never find myself thinking of him... That time I was on the ice with Adam, and Jules was watching, it was like he wasn't there. And yesterday I didn't miss him at all. All that matters is my skating..."

"You've been skating with Adam again since Monday?" This was news to Emma.

"I went yesterday," Jackie said. "I was passing Blades and I went in to say hello to Vikram, and Adam was there and suggested we did a couple of circuits of the ice, as a sort of warm-up to my lesson today. He told me how good I was again; said I should sign up for more lessons."

Emma nodded; that explained why Vikram had told her that he had seen the two of them skating together. She imagined the feel of Adam's strong arm around her waist, and felt a pang of jealousy; what she wouldn't have done to sail across the ice with Adam, as Jackie had done.

"And Adam is so warm and friendly and understanding," Jackie continued. "He's such a nice guy too..."

"You've only known him for a couple of days," Emma pointed out sensibly. "You've known Jules for over two years..."

"Perhaps I've known him for too long," Jackie said sadly. She ran a hand through her long blonde hair. "Sometimes you can know people for a really long time, and still never really know them. But whatever happens, I promise that I'll never do anything to hurt Julian... Just as I'd never hurt you – or Vikram..."

* * *

"You skate wonderfully well, Ms Taylor," Adam said, holding Jackie in his arms as they sped around the rink.

"That's because you're with me," Jackie said, and a shudder of delight ran through her body. "I wouldn't have this sort of confidence by myself!" She grinned, and automatically looked up to the café to see if Vikram was there, before remembering that it was his day off.

Adam took her once more around the rink, helping her to perform a near-perfect figure of eight on the ice, before skating up to the barrier, where they scrunched to a halt. Emma was waiting for them and she gave them a little round of applause as they approached her.

"Pretty classy!" she said.

"Jackie is very good," Adam said, and beamed at Emma, who flushed red with embarrassment and turned away. "I think she should feature in the ice gala at Christmas!"

Jackie smiled, and took her backpack from Emma, who had been holding it while she was on the ice. She drew out her purse, and handed Adam some money – her fee for her half-hour lesson.

"That was really enjoyable, Adam," she said, and shocked herself by giving him a peck on the cheek.

Just a kiss between two new friends, she told herself.

"Even I was impressed," Emma said. She'd seen Jackie's kiss on Adam's cheek: if only she had the nerve to do that! "I've never seen you do such good figures of eight before. If Adam keeps your lessons up you'll be doing double and triple axels next and giving the professionals a run for their money!"

"Maybe you should start doing lessons as well, Emma," Adam suggested encouragingly. "Then you, too, could spin triple axels and do toe jumps and salchows."

He smiled at her again. Emma went weak at the knees.

"Who? Me?" she said, laughing to cover her embarrassment. "I like ice-skating, but I'd never be that good..."

Adam put a hand on Emma's shoulder, just like an older brother. *Well, it certainly wouldn't be like a lover, would it?* Emma thought, as she felt her heart beat faster.

"You shouldn't put yourself down so much," Adam said, his hand still resting on her shoulder. "I've seen you out on the ice – you're good, very good!"

Emma felt herself glowing with pride, and Adam was about to say something else when all three of them became aware of some sort of commotion behind them. They all turned, to see Linsey sweep on to the ice, like some superstar making an entrance for all her adoring fans.

The sexy brunette was wearing an all-in-one Lycra body-suit, which showed off her athletic figure to its best advantage. She was wearing her own skates, and the boots had been polished and repolished until they shone brilliantly in the light.

Every single male at Blades had his eyes glued to her, as she circled the rink in a wide arc, before executing a near-perfect display of skating manoeuvres that left her audience stunned and applauding enthusiastically.

Linsey skated over to the edge of the ice where Jackie, Emma and Adam were watching in astonishment.

"Fancy meeting you two here," she said to Jackie and Emma, before turning all her formidable powers of attraction on Adam. She smiled at him seductively. "Hi," she smouldered. "I'm Linsey. You must be Adam. We've never met but I've watched you loads of times on the ice. I think you're wonderful!"

Adam nodded. "That was a pretty impressive performance out there on the ice too," he remarked.

"Oh *that*!" Linsey said. "It was nothing. I'm sure you could do much, much better..." She hung her head sadly. "Actually there's a part of my technique I'm not too happy with." Here she raised her head and stared at Adam through her dark hooded eyes, suggesting that perhaps she wasn't thinking just of her ice-skating technique. "Perhaps you could help me some time?" she suggested.

"I'd love to," Adam said enthusiastically, and took Linsey's hand. He paused and turned to Jackie and Emma. "Hey, you girls don't mind, do you?"

"Of course not," Emma lied through gritted teeth as she watched Adam and Linsey go off on to the ice hand in hand. As they moved away, Linsey blew them both a sarcastic farewell kiss.

"Can you believe the nerve of that witch!" Jackie hissed as soon as Linsey was out of earshot. "What gives her the right to swan in here, and just take Adam away from us like that?"

Emma shrugged philosophically, and automatically reached up to her own shoulder, feeling the spot where Adam had placed his hand. Just for a moment back there, when he hadn't taken his hand away, she had thought...

Don't be such a little idiot, Emma Carter! she reproved herself. *If he fancies anyone then it's Jackie! Why should a hunk like that think of looking even twice at someone like you!*

"When you look the way Linsey does then I guess that gives you every right," she said. Emma, more so than Jackie, knew what weight sexy good looks could carry with people.

"What's she got against us anyway?" Jackie asked. "We hardly know her and she's acting as though we're arch-enemies."

"Maybe she's just feeling grumpy 'cause she's got the hots for Vik, and he's not showing the slightest bit of interest in her," Emma suggested.

"But why be so horrible to us?" Jackie asked.

"We did tell a little porky-pie to get her off Vik's back," Emma reminded her, and watched Adam and Linsey as they glided around the ice to the sound of one of the summer's biggest hits. "Girls like that never take no for an answer. They're too used to getting their own way. When they don't, they'll take it out on anyone who comes within striking distance. And it looks as though she's picked on you."

"All the same..." Jackie wasn't convinced: how could anyone be that malicious and resentful?

Emma glanced slyly at her friend from out of the corner of her eye. "Who knows? She might think she has some competition..."

"Competition? For Vikram?" Jackie laughed. "Now I know you're talking nonsense, Em! Vik's one of our best mates: we've both known him since we were kids. It's not like either of us to fancy him! Is it?"

"Of course not," smiled Emma, and thought quickly: "But perhaps she sees all females as some sort of obstacle to getting her claws into every single male in sight... And who said that she's just jealous of Vik?" She pointed to the spectators and resting ice-skaters who were standing around the rink, watching Adam and Linsey go through their paces. "Look at the boys – they can't take their eyes off her. And all the girls can't stand the sight of her!"

"You're right," Jackie said, as she gazed at the almost salivating males, and the comic looks of annoyance on their girlfriends' faces. It would almost have been funny were it not for the fact that Jackie felt a deep feeling of apprehension well up somewhere inside her.

Was Linsey really going to continue in her attempts to take Vikram out, and would he finally give in to her advances? Or was she now trying to date Adam? She had certainly come on to the handsome Scandinavian in a pretty heavy way just now, and Adam was clearly impressed with the girl's ice-skating skills.

And why are you getting so worried and hot under the collar about it anyway, Jackie Taylor? she scolded herself, although in her heart of hearts she suspected she knew the reason why. *Linsey can do whatever she wants, and it shouldn't bother you in the slightest – after all, it's not as though she's after Julian!...*

Yet...

She turned back to Emma. "She's vile," Jackie stated categorically, and chuckled at her audacity: she rarely had a bad word to say about anyone.

"Not to the boys she isn't," Emma added.

Jackie nodded. "Still, I bet she hasn't got many girlfriends," she said. "They must all hate her."

"Jackie," Emma said, with all the world-weary wisdom of a seventeen-year-old who thought she was much too plain, and would never get a boyfriend, "You saw her the other night in Slinky Jo's with all those trendy boys. With the sort of looks Linsey has do you think she cares how few girlfriends she has?"

A few days later, Jackie was skating on the ice, getting warmed up ready for her lesson with Adam, when she spotted Vikram standing on the edge of the rink. He waved at her, slightly awkwardly, as though he had just been caught spying on someone. She skated over to him; they kissed each other on the cheek, as they always did.

Jackie stepped off the ice, and sat next to him on one of the wooden benches. They were so close that their legs were touching, Vikram's black 501s brushing against her bare skin.

Two young girls, no more than twelve years old, passed by on their way to the café and looked Vikram up and down with all the studied appraisal of a pair of pre-pubescents out on a hunk-hunt. They liked what they saw – firm muscles, lithe body, and thick raven locks to run their fingers through – and giggled to themselves all the way up the stairs. Jackie smiled after them – they'd probably assumed she was Vikram's girlfriend – although Vik appeared not to have noticed them.

"How long have you been watching?" she asked.

"Ten minutes or so," Vikram said. "It's my lunch hour."

"I can think of better things to do in your break," Jackie said. "It's nice and sunny outside; you could go for a walk in the park, or even drop in at Slinky Jo's for a cappuccino."

"Nope," he said, and laughed. "I'd be bound to run into Linsey there! Whenever she's not out on the ice, she seems always to be there."

"Like a spider in its web," Jackie joked.

"An exceptionally pretty spider, all the same," was Vikram's opinion, and for just one half-instant Jackie's face fell into a mask of despair, "if you like that sort of thing," he finished and Jackie brightened up.

"Is she still chasing after you?" she asked, trying to sound casual and nonchalant.

Vikram nodded. "Not as much as she used to, but I suspect she's not the sort of girl who gives up easily," he said. "I suppose it's flattering in a way – although goodness knows why she's interested in me."

Because everyone says that you're the hunkiest, sexiest and most desirable male in town! Jackie thought, but said: "Maybe we should buy her a white stick and a guide dog?"

Vikram laughed and attempted to give Jackie a friendly cuff on the chin. Jackie raised a hand to defend herself, grabbed Vikram's strong, masculine hand and held it in her own, lacing her fingers in his. She felt her hand tingle, as though volts of electricity were being passed from Vikram to her. They looked at each other curiously, in a way that two friends would never look at each other.

Slowly Jackie lowered Vikram's hand, placing it back on his thigh. Still their hands remained clasped for a moment; and then Jackie hurriedly took hers away. She looked away from Vikram, at the other skaters on the ice: Adam was there, taking one of his students around the rink.

"Anyway, I like watching the skaters," Vikram said after a pause. "And you're very good, you know... I often see you from the café up there..."

"Yes, I know you do," she said. "I always look up to see if you're there watching me..."

"It looks fun."

"You should try it."

"Who? Me?" Vikram laughed. "You know I've got two left feet."

"I remember dancing with you at college discos," Jackie recalled. "By the end of the evening my feet were black and blue from the number of times you stepped on them!" She stood up and took Vikram's hand again, pulling him to his feet.

"Hey, what are you doing?" he laughed, as he allowed himself to be taken to the rink's office.

"Vikram Pandy, you are going to go ice-skating!" Jackie announced, as she hired a pair of size-ten skating boots and blades from the office and handed them over to Vikram. "It's crazy you working in the café and not being able to spend your lunchtimes skating!"

"Look, Jackie, I'm not so sure that this is a good idea," Vikram said doubtfully as he sat down and pulled on and laced up his boots.

"Nonsense," Jackie said and, grasping Vikram's hand once again, she led him to the edge of the rink. Unused to the unfamiliar skating boots and their blades, Vikram waddled across the rubber-matted floor towards the ice looking for all the world like a penguin. Jackie found it a struggle not to laugh. Vikram was usually so cool and collected, a trendy, great-looking smoothie; it was great fun to see him so defenceless for a change! And her heart leapt out for him in his sudden vulnerability, as she realized that all she wanted to do was to be there for him, by his side, helping and supporting him, whenever he needed her, for ever.

But just as friends, of course.

Jackie stepped on to the ice, and turned to look at Vikram who was regarding the slippery surface without much enthusiasm. "It's perfectly safe," she said.

Vikram didn't believe her. "You would say that, wouldn't you?" he said. "I've a terrible sense of balance at the best of times. How do you think I'm going to stay upright on two stainless steel blades less than a quarter of an inch thick?"

Jackie grinned, relishing Vikram's dilemma. "Don't be such a softie, Vik," she said. "When have I ever let you down?"

"Lots of times," he confirmed. "Starting from when we were kids together and you nicked my last Smartie!"

"Aha, but I'm not a little girl any more!"

"No, you're not…"

Jackie placed Vikram's hand on the handrail which encircled the entire rink. "Keep a grip of that," she said, "and you won't fall. And I'll be holding you as well: I won't let you make a fool of yourself."

"That a promise?" he asked warily, and he gripped the handrail with his right hand, while, on his left, Jackie encircled his slim waist with her arm.

"That's a promise!" she said, and started to move slowly along the ice. Vikram tried to follow her, making the same sort of faltering steps as a baby would on "dry" land.

Jackie tut-tutted. "You're on the ice, dimwit!" she teased. "You don't walk – you glide." She looked down at Vikram's two left feet, and instructed him to place them in the form of a "T". "Now, just push with your front foot and then follow with your back one – it's easy!"

Indeed, under Jackie's patient tuition Vikram did find it surprisingly easy, and within minutes the two of them were circling the ice – slowly certainly, and very unsteadily, as Vikram was still half-holding the safety rail, while Jackie's arm was wrapped tightly round his waist (and his around hers).

"Hey, you know this is quite good fun," Vikram said, and looked down into Jackie's eyes.

"The best," said Jackie. "I love the sense of freedom and – whoops! Watch out!"

Vikram had almost lost his balance as they took a particularly sharp curve, and, for a couple of seconds, both of them tottered until they regained their centre of gravity.

Jackie was enjoying her skating immensely, and, even more than that, she was having a great time showing off to Vikram. His lack of skill on the ice gave her confidence in her own abilities, far more confidence than Adam's repeated assurances of her talent had given her. And, looking up into Vikram's happy but nervous face, she saw an expression she had never seen before: Vikram, normally so confident, so powerful and reliable, now looked as helpless as a child learning to walk.

Vikram was depending on her, he needed her, she suddenly realized, and that was a new feeling for both of them. Jackie had never experienced anyone relying on her before: even Julian could get along very well without her, thank you very much, and if anyone was in an inferior position in that relationship then it was Jackie. Julian constantly gave her presents, and did things for her, but there was never anything that she could do for him. But here on the ice, Vikram had placed all his trust in her: it felt good to be needed, she decided.

"See, I told you it was easy!" she grinned at him,

and felt his arm tighten its hold on her waist. "I knew you'd get the hang of it in –"

Vikram yelped, and lost his balance, crashing to the floor. In a panic he grabbed hold of Jackie's free arm, and tried to pull himself up. With a shriek Jackie lost her balance too, and smashed down on to the floor on top of Vikram, much to the delight of several spectators. At the far end of the ice, Adam, who was still with his younger pupil, turned around and grinned.

"Easy, huh?" Vikram grunted sarcastically, and found himself staring right into Jackie's eyes – hardly surprising as her face was only an inch away from his. "You told me I could trust you!"

"First rule of ice-skating: trust no one. And the second rule is never grab hold of another skater when you've just decided to make an idiot of yourself," Jackie giggled. "It's not particularly dignified doing a prat-fall on the ice – especially when yours truly wants to make a good impression on her tutor!"

"Not dignified, huh?" Vikram joked. "It feels pretty 'dignified' from where I am!"

He shut up abruptly. He had gone too far, said too much, and suddenly the joke was no longer a joke. He stared up into Jackie's eyes; her long blonde hair flopped down and swung over his mouth. He tasted Jackie's freshness on his lips, smelt her natural fragrance. They were so near that they could hear each other's breathing, feel the beat of each other's hearts.

Jackie felt a pair of strong arms lift her off Vikram and help her stand up. The same pair of arms then restored Vikram to his upright (if very wobbly) position.

"So when my back's turned you're two-timing me with my best friend?" Julian cracked, and gave Jackie a peck on the cheek.

"Julian, it's not like that at all!" Jackie protested, and Julian laughed.

"Of course it's not," he said, and glanced sideways at Vikram. "Vik would never try to steal you away from me. Would you, big buddy?"

"Of course not," said Vikram, and smiled nervously.

"Besides he's already spoken for, from all accounts," Julian added and realized, when Vikram glowered evilly at him, that he'd hit a raw nerve by reminding him about his forthcoming arranged marriage to Lakshmi.

"What do you mean?" Jackie asked and looked questioningly at Vikram.

"Skip it," he said, and started to stagger off the ice.

Jackie looked questioningly at Julian: there was a secret here, she would ask Julian about it later.

Julian took a small envelope from the back pocket of his Chinos, and presented it to Jackie, who looked at it curiously. She opened it: it was a pair of tickets for the next Powerhouse concert.

"Call it my way of saying sorry for the other night," he said, "when I stormed off the ice. It's been bugging me for a couple of days now – I was way out of order then."

"It's me who should be sorry," Jackie insisted.

"I shouldn't have stood you up like that on Wednesday just for my silly old ice-skating class."

"It's OK," Julian said, and he tried to forget how he had also let Jackie down the previous Saturday. "I should have realized that you wanted your own space. And if Adam's right and you could make that Christmas gala then it's important for you."

Jackie leaned forward and kissed Julian on the lips. "Thanks, Jules, you're so good to me," she said. "So understanding."

Julian held Jackie in his arms. "It's entirely my pleasure," he told her. "I do love you, Jackie."

Jackie smiled, wanting to tell Julian that yes, she loved him too, and wondering why she couldn't bring herself to say the words. She glanced over his shoulder: on the ice Adam had finished his lesson, and he was skating up to them. She released herself from Julian's embrace.

"I have to go now," she said, "it's time for my lesson."

Julian smiled understandingly. "And afterwards we can go out, maybe to Slinky Jo's?"

"Yes, of course, Jules, that would be wonderful," Jackie said half-heartedly, and went off to join Adam for her lesson.

But Jackie had learnt a lesson in those few minutes, a lesson which had just changed her life for ever.

7

Jackie looked at herself in the bathroom mirror, and nodded approvingly. She was wearing her favourite leather jacket (a present from Julian for her last birthday), tight black 501s and boots, and a baggy white shirt. Her blonde hair had been swept back, and her make-up was subtle but effective, with just a hint of glitter on her eyelids. She knew that she looked a million dollars for the Powerhouse concert and, as she checked her pockets for her money, she felt the two tickets that Julian had bought: they were in the front row, naturally: nothing was too good for Julian.

Jackie and Julian used to love going to rock gigs, losing themselves in the music, and the company of other fun-loving people. *Perhaps tonight some of that old magic would return*, she thought hopefully, *perhaps tonight she would realize that Julian really was the man for her*. She smiled, as her mind turned its attentions, unbidden, to Vikram. Vik hated Powerhouse, calling them a "bunch of talentless goons": there'd certainly be no danger of bumping into him tonight!

Jackie was about to go downstairs to wait for the taxi that Julian had said he would order for her, when the phone rang. Frowning – she wasn't expecting a call at this time – she picked up the receiver.

"Hello?"

"Hi, Jackie, it's me," Julian introduced himself at the end of the line. As soon as she heard Julian's voice, Jackie felt her heart sink.

"What's up?" Jackie asked, even though she had a fair idea.

"Jackie, I'm really sorry, but I can't make it tonight," Julian said.

Jackie sighed. Somehow she'd had a feeling that this was coming. "Why not, Julian?" she asked peevishly. "What's wrong?"

There was a pause at the other end, before Julian said that he had an emergency assignment for college, which he had to hand in the first day of the forthcoming term. It couldn't be put off and might even go some way to helping him get a place at medical school next year.

"But I've already rung up Emma," he said quickly before Jackie could say anything. "She's more than happy to go with you tonight: I told her to come straight round to your place..."

You've got it all tied up nicely, haven't you, Jules? Jackie found herself thinking. *But what are you really up to? Is it another girl? Or is it that you just don't want to see me?*

"Look, Jackie, you don't know how sorry I am," Julian said. "But I promise you, I'll make it up to you."

"Yes, Julian, I'm sure you will," Jackie said coldly. "You always do..."

With a heavy heart she hung up the phone, just as Emma rang the front door bell. On the other end of the line, Julian replaced the receiver and sighed. It was all a lie, of course. But there was no other girl, there wasn't even an emergency assignment. It was simply that, much as he cared for Jackie, he just didn't want to see her tonight. What was happening to him, he wondered. Why could he not admit the truth to himself and to Jackie: he no longer loved her the way he once had.

And yet to see Jackie hurt would break Julian's heart...

"Look, I'm really sorry I couldn't make it, Jackie," Julian said a few nights later when they all met up in Slinky Jo's.

"Oh, that's quite all right," Jackie said icily. "You buy me tickets for the hottest gig of the year and then you don't turn up!"

"I had a lot of studying to do," Julian claimed. "And it's not as though I stood you up – I let you know beforehand, didn't I?"

"And am I ever glad you did, Jules!" gushed Emma. "Jackie and I had a great time. That lead singer is just so hunky!"

"I really am sorry, Jackie," Julian repeated. "But you know how important my work is..." He took her hands in his.

"I know, Jules," Jackie said, unwilling to continue the argument; in fact she hadn't had a passionate argument with Julian for months now. "But sometimes I just wish..." Her voice trailed off.

"Wish what, Jackie?"

I just wish that I could feel something when your hands touch mine, that's all, Jackie thought.

"Oh, nothing," she said.

"Forgiven?" Julian asked and winked at her with those pretty-boy eyes of his. How could anyone resist them?

"Forgiven," Jackie smiled, and stood up to go. She and Emma were going down to Blades. Did he want to come? Julian shook his head, reminding Jackie just how unsteady he was on the ice. The girls laughed and left.

"OK, so what's up, Julian?" asked Vikram after Jackie and Emma had left Slinky Jo's.

"What d'you mean, 'what's up'?" his friend asked, although he knew perfectly well what Vikram was talking about. He looked around the café: a group of exceptionally pretty girls were sitting around one of the nearby tables, laughing and joking and sharing a jug of sangria. When they caught sight of Julian looking at them they started to giggle. Julian reached out for his own glass of wine, but Vikram moved it away, making Julian turn around and look at him.

"Standing Jackie up like that," Vikram said. "That's the second time you've done it in as many weeks with no apparent reason at all."

Julian took his glass and gulped at his wine. "I told you," he said, "I've got lots of studying to do."

Vikram shook his head. "Sorry, Jules," he said. "Jackie might fall for that but not me. So why are you lying to Jackie?"

Julian gritted his teeth in an effort to control his temper. What gave Vikram the right to probe him about his personal life like this?

"Look, I just wanted some time to myself, that's all," he said finally. "We see each other practically every single day."

"Because you invite her out," Vikram reminded him. "And then you get cold feet and come up with these wild excuses to cancel. As if you don't really want to see her any more."

"Hey, stop hassling me, Vik," Julian pleaded. "I've got my reasons."

"So tell them to Jackie," Vikram urged him. "I'm sure she'd understand."

"And I'm sure you don't understand women," Julian snapped. "She'd automatically assume that I'm carrying on with someone behind her back – someone like Linsey maybe."

"And are you?" Vikram challenged.

"No," was Julian's firm reply. "I'd never two-time Jackie. I ... I love her..."

"We all do."

"What?" Julian stared accusingly at Vikram, and Vik realized that he had said too much.

"As a friend, I mean," he said hastily. "We all love Jackie as a friend."

Julian looked thoughtfully at his mate for a moment, before saying: "Yeah, well, I love her as more than a friend – I love her as my girlfriend..."

Well, you sure have a funny way of showing it, thought Vikram.

"This is quite a surprise, Jackie," Adam said, as he settled back into the plush seating of the sushi bar, having devoured an enormous bowl of noodles.

"I was at a loose end tonight, so I came to the rink on the off-chance of seeing if you were free," she said.

"And I was!" Adam laughed. "But I certainly didn't expect to be taken out for a slap-up candle-lit Japanese meal by one of my students! You spend enough money already on your classes!"

"They're worth every penny, and besides, the record store pays good money," Jackie said and sipped at her glass of sake (Adam had ordered it, and she hadn't wanted to tell him that she didn't like the taste). "Especially if you think I'll be good enough to take part in the Christmas gala," she added uncertainly.

"Of course you will be," Adam said and rested his hand on hers. He laughed: "With me as your teacher you can't fail!"

Jackie looked down at Adam's hand, and her head started swimming in a sea of conflicting emotions, and an awful feeling of guilt. There was something wrong with her relationship with Julian, she was beginning to realize now, and that was why she was reaching out for Adam, just as earlier the thought of Vikram had fired her body with strange new feelings. What was she doing here with this man, when she knew that Julian was working hard at home, in his efforts to set up some sort of future for them? And what would Vikram think if – if – well, what did it matter what Vikram thought? He was her friend, that was all.

Wasn't he?

Vikram didn't place his hand on hers, Vikram didn't hold her tightly round the waist when they circled the ice, like equals. Vikram had been there for ever, as much a part of her life as her mother, her family, her friends. Adam was something new and exciting in her life, with his Scandinavian-American accent, and the way he made her feel so confident out there on the ice.

She glanced up: Adam was smiling at her now, and the candlelight caught in his long blond hair, making it shine and glisten like finely-spun gold. His steely blue eyes sparkled in the light.

Adam was one of the most attractive men she had ever seen, Jackie suddenly realized, possessing cool good looks which reminded her of snow at Christmas, or beautiful frost-patterns on a window pane. His beauty was so different from Julian's sandy-haired boyish looks; and a million miles away from Vikram's wild and brooding darkness.

"I hope you're not just my teacher, Adam," she breathed softly. "I hope you're also my friend."

"Of course I am," Adam reassured her warmly.

Moments passed, as Jackie struggled with her emotions, painfully aware that Adam, this man who was so different to Julian, had not yet taken his hand away from hers. Finally, she closed her eyes and leant forward to kiss Adam lightly on the lips. She felt Adam tense, and draw back; he took his hand away from hers.

Jackie opened her eyes, and saw the look of surprise on Adam's face, and instantly realized her mistake.

Adam smiled. "Jackie, I think you've got your wires crossed somewhere," he said, not unkindly.

Jackie suddenly felt like the biggest fool ever. She wished the ground would open up beneath her. "I ... I thought..." she stammered, and then found that there were no words to express what she felt.

"Hey, it's OK," Adam said. "It's a natural mistake to make."

"I just thought ... it felt so good skating with you, having you hold me in your arms," Jackie said. She grimaced. "I guess I've just made a right idiot of myself, haven't I? Just like a little kid, having a crush on the teacher!"

"You're not a little kid, Jackie – you're only a couple of years younger than me," Adam said. "And like you said, I'm not just your teacher – I also hope I'll be your friend. It's just that you're not my type –"

"Well, thank you very much," Jackie quipped in a half-successful attempt to relieve the tension.

"And you have a boyfriend – Julian," Adam continued. "And somehow you don't seem to me to be the sort of person to cheat on him."

Jackie sighed. "It feels so right when we're going round the ice together, you holding me by the waist," she said. "Feeling your touch. It's just so different..."

"Different?"

"Julian hardly ever holds me now, not the way you do..." she said. "When he touches me it no longer means anything... There's no thrill, no excitement, no passion..."

"He seems to love you very much indeed," Adam said. "Vikram and Emma tell me that he's always giving you presents."

Jackie grimaced. "Yeah, the most expensive clothes, the trendiest CDs, tickets for the hottest gigs," she said. "But that's not what love is, is it? It's not about material things, or possessions, or getting the biggest present for your birthday. Sometimes I think that he's trying to buy me off with all those presents..."

"'Buy you off'? What d'you mean?"

"It's as if that's the only way he can express his feelings for me," she said. "Whenever he cancels a date for whatever reason, I know for sure that he'll give me an expensive gift the next day to make up for it. But how many times have you seen him hold me on the rink, or kiss me anywhere other than on the cheek?"

"I take your point," Adam said.

"He doesn't hold me the way he used to when we first started going out," Jackie despaired. "He's not as tender as he used to be... At times he seems to be far away, on another planet."

"He seemed pretty upset when you cancelled your date to take your first skating lesson," Adam pointed out.

“That was just his silly pride,” Jackie decided. “And he apologized for it afterwards –”

“With another present?”

Jackie nodded.

Adam reached out for Jackie’s hands again, and she let him take them. There was no misunderstanding this time: she realized that this was just Adam’s way of showing affection, of making contact with people – he had no ulterior motive.

“How long have you been going out with Julian?” he asked.

“Two years – three years next January,” she replied.

“People change, Jackie,” Adam said. “And when they do there are no heroes and no villains. Sometimes they just grow out of love with each other. It’s sad, but that’s the way it is. And it’s hard and painful to break out of that love, but you have to do it.”

“But how do I know, Adam?” she asked. “How do I know if I have grown out of love with Julian?”

Adam looked kindly at her, a knowing smile on his face. “I could tell you,” he said, “but it’s up to you to find out for yourself...”

Jackie smiled back, aware that she had made a new friend. It seemed odd telling a boy all her troubles, but there was something trustworthy about Adam which inspired confidence.

It was the same sort of confidence that enabled her to skate so well when she was with him. They made a team, she realized, and even though Adam was a much better skater than her, on the ice he brought out the best in her. On the ice they were equals, partners, each relying on the other: neither one inferior to the other, neither one superior. That was what friendship was all about, Jackie realized; but what was love all about?

Did she still really love Julian, she wondered. There was an aching deep inside her, she knew that; and if she truly had fallen out of love with Julian then she knew that it would break his heart – and she couldn't do that, could she? She shook her head, and looked at Adam, misty-eyed.

"You're wrong, Adam," she said. "Julian is so kind to me, so generous, I do love him, I really do love him."

Adam smiled kindly. "I'm sure you do, Jackie," he said. "But are you *in* love with him?"

And Jackie no longer knew the answer.

Jackie and Adam stayed in the restaurant for another half hour, happy that they had reached a new understanding. Adam was a charmer, of that there was no doubt, but, as he had said, he needed to be if he had to convince what he called the ice-skating mothers to pay good money to send their spoilt daughters to his lessons.

Bizarrely, as Adam talked, Jackie found her mind returning to Vikram, as she realized just how different Adam was to Vikram, who simply wasn't aware of the devastating effect he had on the opposite sex. Vikram with his muscular physique, and the way his chest hairs peeked out over the top of his T-shirts sometimes; his firm jawline, and his million-dollar smile which could turn even the dreariest October day into the first day of the summer holidays. The way he never went out to impress anyone, or put on an act, and was always himself; but was invariably polite and considerate, even with pushy little witches like Linsey. Kind, intelligent and straightforward, with the proportions of a Greek god: the spotty little kid from next door, on whose shoulder she used to cry, had turned into a prize catch for some lucky girl, and the crazy thing was that he didn't even realize it himself!

And while there was now no doubting Adam's sincerity in his friendship with her, she still found Vikram's unassuming manner preferable and his good looks all the more appealing because of his total ignorance of them. Whoever Vikram eventually fell in love with would be one lucky girl, she decided.

As they left the sushi bar, they failed to notice Linsey who had just arrived, with her usual entourage of trendy and good-looking boys and girls. Linsey, however, noticed them, and scowled when she spotted Adam helping Jackie on with her coat.

She saw red. She'd had her eyes on Adam, ever since she'd realized she was on a losing streak with Vikram, and thought she had made a start by impressing him out on the ice. And now here Jackie was, stealing the hunky ice-skater right from under her nose!

Quivering with fury and jealousy, Linsey plotted her revenge.

8

As the evening drew to a close, the music in the trendy club, to which Julian had taken Jackie, changed to a slower and sexier beat. The two of them looked at each other as if to say: *Shall we?*

All around them other couples were pairing off for the last slow-dance of the night. They'd both look fools, they silently decided, if they joined the other couples who were slinking off to the bar, embarrassed, or unwilling to indulge in some decidedly untrendy and intimate touch-dancing. Jackie and Julian were boyfriend and girlfriend; sharing the last dance of the night was only what was to be expected of them.

Julian put his arms around Jackie, pressing his warm body hard against hers, and Jackie reached up to run her fingers through his fine, sandy-blond hair. They swayed dreamily to the music, and Jackie rested her head on his shoulder, watching the other smooching couples on the dance floor.

Over by the bar, Vikram was chatting to a

couple of his mates, and ordering a low-alcohol cider from the pretty barmaid: it was obvious that she was very attracted to him.

Obvious to everyone apart from Vik, Jackie realized, as her handsome friend – *my handsome friend, and that's all!* – took the drink from the girl, barely acknowledging her, and continued chatting with his mates. No doubt they were debating the merits of various football teams, she decided. Vikram hadn't come with her and Julian to the disco, but it had been a pleasant surprise when they had run into him; for the first hour they hadn't danced, but had just sat chatting.

"Are you happy?"

The voice seemed to come from a long way away, and Jackie looked up at Julian.

"Sorry?" she asked.

"I asked you if you're happy," Julian said, and ran his fingers distractedly up and down Jackie's spine. Jackie smiled, and gave a brief sigh of pleasure; after all, that was what girls were supposed to do when boys as handsome as Julian massaged the hollow of their back, wasn't it?

"Of course, I am," Jackie said, and kissed Julian briefly on the lips. "It's been a lovely evening, Jules. I've really enjoyed myself."

It wasn't a lie, Julian certainly knew how to give a girl a good time: he had picked her up in a cab, taken her to a new exclusive restaurant where he had blown his father's money on a candlelit dinner for two, and then taken her to the trendiest of clubs in town. Jackie calculated that he must have spent a small fortune on her.

"I just wanted to make tonight really special for you," Julian said, and glanced over to the pretty barmaid who was making eyes at Vikram, before turning back to his girlfriend. "We seem to be seeing less of each other lately – I was wondering whether there was something wrong..."

For a second Jackie froze almost perceptibly in Julian's arms, and then resumed moving back and forth to the music.

"Of course there isn't," she said. "It's just that I've been so tied up with my ice-skating recently, that I haven't had time to go out." It had been three weeks now since she had had her chat with Adam in the sushi bar, and he had been constantly encouraging her in her skating, saying that she had a lot of talent.

"Maybe I should be jealous of Adam?" Julian said, but when he saw the worried look on Jackie's face, he smiled, and kissed her on the forehead. "Hey, it's just a joke," he claimed. "I realize I was wrong when I thought that you preferred your ice-skating tutor to me!"

Jackie stopped dancing, and shrugged herself out of Julian's arms. *Did he suspect something?* she asked herself, and then considered. But what was there to suspect? After all, there was nothing going on between her and Adam and there never would be.

"Hey, what's up, Jackie?" Julian asked.

"Nothing, Jules," she said. "I'm just tired of dancing now. Shall we sit this one out?"

"Whatever you say," Julian said indulgently, and allowed Jackie to take his hand and lead him off the dance floor. They threaded their way through the dancing couples, and back to the bar and Vikram. He smiled when he saw them, and Jackie took her hand away from Julian's.

"Touch-dancing!" he scoffed with a look of disgust on his face. "How yukky can you get?"

"Some romantic you are, best buddy," said Julian, and accepted a glass of cider from him. "You'll never know how good it is until you try it!"

"Alas, I have no fair maiden like Jackie to dance with!" Vikram moaned theatrically.

"I'm sure Jackie wouldn't mind dancing with you," Julian said, all innocence. "Would you, Jackie?"

A beat. A brief exchange of glances between Jackie and Vikram. And then: "Of course not."

"It doesn't matter," Vikram said quickly. "I don't really want to dance at all..."

Julian looked strangely from Vikram to Jackie and then back at Vikram again. "What is it with you two?" he asked finally. "You're both about as jumpy as each other!"

"I ... I twisted my ankle playing football tonight," Vikram lied. "I couldn't dance even if I wanted to..."

Julian made sympathetic noises. "Tough luck, Vik," he said. "I guess it was Jake Bond's fault, huh? He's a mean mother when he's playing."

"Er, that's right," Vikram said, and made a mental note to get Jake to back him up on his alibi. "I guess he's never forgiven me for refusing to take his sister Clare out on a date!"

"The poor girl must have been devastated,"

came a familiar voice, and they turned to see a flash of scarlet and black designer clothes. Linsey had spotted them and had come over in order, so she said, to say goodnight.

Pull the other one! Jackie thought.

"Oh, hi, Linsey," Vikram said, as she pecked him on the cheek, as she would a friend. It was hard to think that only a few weeks ago she was practically throwing herself at him. Linsey turned and acknowledged Jackie pleasantly, which immediately set Jackie's alarm bells ringing.

And then Linsey looked at Julian, fixing all her sultry charms on him. "I haven't seen you down at Blades recently," she said, casually.

"I've been catching up on some work," Julian said and smiled. "It's Jackie who's the skating champ around here."

"Of course," Linsey said. "She and Adam look so good together on the ice – real partners. I guess it's because they get on so well socially too. I see them all over the place, at Slinky Jo's, at that trendy sushi bar on the high street –"

Julian frowned. He'd been out with Jackie and Emma and Adam occasionally to Slinky Jo's, but never to the sushi bar.

"Oh, about three weeks ago now, I think it was," Linsey said sweetly, as though butter wouldn't melt in her mouth. Jackie glared hatefully at her.

"You didn't mention this to me," Julian said to Jackie.

"I must have forgotten," Jackie said, who had purposely not let Julian know of her meal with

Adam out of embarrassment. "It wasn't important anyway."

Linsey put a hand on Jackie's shoulder. "Oh dear, Emma –"

"It's Jackie."

"Of course it is; how silly of me to forget. I haven't dropped you in it, have I?" she asked, and, before Jackie could reply, she took her hand from Jackie and offered it to Julian. "Don't get the wrong idea," she said. "There was nothing out of order about it."

"Of course not," Julian said. "Jackie isn't like that."

A bizarre thought sped through Jackie's mind: *how dare he take me so much for granted?*

"Especially not with someone as handsome as you are," Linsey smarmed, and finally took her hand off Julian, satisfied that she had sown a seed of doubt in his mind. And with that she made her excuses and left them standing at the bar.

"She's a nice girl," Julian said, and Jackie looked curiously at him.

"And how would you know?" she teased.

Julian coloured. "I've seen her at the ice rink when I've been watching you," he said.

"You couldn't miss her in those tarty clothes," Jackie said, unkindly but truthfully.

"I think she's lonely," Julian said thoughtfully, and watched Linsey's departing figure – along with most of the other men in the place. "She's always by herself."

"No, she just doesn't have any friends – real friends anyway – 'cause she's so unpleasant to people – other girls at least," Jackie said. "Look at the way she latches on to anyone's boyfriend – even Vik here!"

"What do you mean, 'even Vik here'?" Vikram asked, and laughed. "I have been able to pass as quite presentable-looking occasionally!"

Gorgeous-looking, more like, Jackie thought.

My gorgeous-looking friend.

"Anyway, Vikram isn't anyone's boyfriend," Julian said, as if Jackie needed any reminding. "And Linsey hasn't been giving him the eye like she used to..."

"Alas, she has decided that I'm a lost cause!" Vikram chuckled, and then slapped his mate on the back. "It seems, however, that she thinks you're a different case!"

The atmosphere froze, and Jackie and Julian exchanged worried looks. It was as if Vikram had unwittingly put his finger on a truth neither of them had been willing to admit. When he noticed the effect of his words, Vikram clapped his hands together, in an attempt to change the subject.

"Enough of psycho-analysing man-mad Linsey!" he said. "Let's make arrangements for tomorrow night. We're all still going to see this dreary old movie, aren't we?"

Earlier that day, Jackie and Julian, Vikram and Emma, had all agreed to go to the cinema to see one of the latest blockbusters the following night. It was, so Emma read from the reviews in the local newspaper while sitting in Blades café, "a tender and haunting vision of romance and betrayal and a passion that wouldn't die". Vikram had replied that, if it was all the same to them, couldn't they just go and see the latest blood 'n' gore sci-fi action fest instead?

Emma had shook her head firmly, and declared that it wasn't surprising he didn't have a girlfriend if that was his taste in movies. Vikram had finally conceded, after some brow-beating from Jackie and Emma, even though Julian had been mildly on his side.

"Of course," Jackie said.

Vikram sighed. "I was thinking perhaps you'd changed your mind," he said dolefully, and looked at Julian, hoping for some loyal masculine support.

"You never know, you might enjoy it, Vik," Julian laughed, betraying Vikram's faith in him. "It's even up for some Oscars!"

"Big deal!"

Jackie joined in Julian's teasing of Vikram. "You've just no soul, Vik," she said. "You've got no heart, no sense of romance!"

"Oh yes I have," he replied.

There was a momentary pause in the friends' chatter, unnoticed only by Julian.

"So prove it, Vik!" Julian said. "Be at the cinema at seven-thirty tomorrow as arranged! Afterwards we can go on to Slinky Jo's – it'll be my treat."

Vikram rammed his hands into the pockets of his Chinos, and affected a pretty convincing sulk. "If I have to..." he grumbled. "Although give me an Arnie actioner any day!"

Julian smiled, and looked at his watch: it was almost one-thirty in the morning. It was time to go home, he said, and, despite Jackie's protests that she could get a cab, he insisted that he take her home. He reached out to put an arm around her waist, and then turned to Vikram.

"You want a lift too?" he asked. "After all, you're practically Jackie's next-door neighbour."

Vikram smiled gratefully. "Thanks, but no thanks. You two will want to be alone," he said; was it regret that Jackie could detect in his voice? "I'll walk it. It's not far and I've got some thinking to do."

"Have it your own way," Julian said, unconcerned by Vikram's sudden change of mood. He started to walk off with Jackie towards the exit. As they left, Jackie turned and saw Vikram, who was watching them go.

Suddenly he looked so alone, so vulnerable, surrounded as he was by kissing and dancing couples, or laughing boys at the bar. There was a look of yearning on his face, and of sadness too, as though he would break down at any moment into tears of longing and regret. Her heart went out to him, and Jackie suddenly knew that she didn't want to go home, that she wanted to stay here with her friend, with Vikram.

"C'mon, Jackie, it's getting late!" said her boyfriend, and, casting one last look behind her, Jackie let herself be escorted out of the club.

9

"You're doing really well, Emma," Adam approved the following day as Emma executed a perfect figure of eight on the ice under Adam's critical gaze. She came to a halt and beamed gratefully at the handsome skating instructor.

"You really think so?" she said.

"I wouldn't say so if I didn't mean it," he said truthfully. "Ever since I started teaching you, you've improved by leaps and bounds."

Emma gulped: was this impossibly handsome Viking actually speaking to her and complimenting her? And was it her imagination or was he really spending more and more time with her, stretching her lessons out more than the quarter-hours she had paid for? Of course it was her imagination: she would have to be a fool to think that someone as gorgeous as Adam could be attracted to someone like her!

"I've loved ice-skating since I was little but I've always been such a klutz before," she admitted. "If I have improved then it's all down to you!"

Adam chuckled as he took her hand and skated with her towards the edge of the ice; it was the end of their session and he had another lesson to take in a couple of minutes.

"Jackie said something very similar a couple of weeks ago!" he remembered. "I'm afraid all this praise is going to go to my head!"

When they reached the barrier, Emma stopped and sighed. "But even with all your teaching I'm never going to be as good as Linsey," she complained. "Or as pretty," she added.

Like a good mate, Adam chucked Emma under the chin. "Linsey's a great skater if something of a show-off," he said. "And what if she is conventionally attractive? Some men don't like their women to be sizzling sex-bombs –"

"Aha! So you have noticed then!"

"– They know that beauty's only skin-deep," Adam finished. "It's what a person is like underneath that really counts. Their wit, their intelligence, their personality – not how many heads they can turn on the ice or when they're walking down the high street."

There was a pause, and, for want of anything better, Emma looked at her watch – six o'clock – and then asked: "Where is Linsey for that matter? She's usually on the ice by this time, putting on a show for all those sex-crazed pimply adolescents who come here to ogle and drool over her."

Adam shrugged. "I never even noticed she wasn't here," he said. "I've been watching you all the time!"

"Yeah, well, you are my teacher, aren't you?" she

said. *After all, why else would a hunk like Adam want to look at a frizzy-haired, plain Jane like me?* she thought.

"Of course, that's all I am – just your teacher," Adam confirmed, and kissed Emma goodbye as she went off to the girls' changing rooms to take off her skating boots and have a shower.

Adam skated back into the centre of the ice, and looked around for his next pupil, a nine-year-old girl who, in common with most of his other pupils, was hopelessly in love with her Scandinavian skating instructor. She hadn't yet arrived, and as he circled the ice, he spied Julian waving at him from the side. He skated over to him.

Julian was dressed smartly in a pair of freshly-pressed Chinos, and a black unstructured designer jacket which had probably cost him – or rather his father's credit card – more than Adam earned in a month. He was also carrying a rolled-up umbrella: it was raining outside.

Julian nodded briefly to him: while he had now realized that Adam was no threat to his relationship with Jackie, and had indeed shared a cappuccino with him a couple of times, the two boys weren't particularly good mates. (In truth, Julian was a little jealous of the admiring looks which Adam, a far better skater than he would ever be, received from the girls at Blades.)

"Is Jackie here?" he asked, and Adam shook his head: he hadn't seen her all day. "I tried contacting her at home but there was no reply."

"Is there something wrong?" Adam asked: there was an anxious look on Julian's face.

"Er ... no ... well, yes, as a matter of fact there is," Julian said guiltily. "I'm supposed to be meeting her, Emma and Vikram tonight at the cinema," he continued, and mentioned the romantic film they were all planning to see.

"And you can't make it?" Adam guessed, and looked searchingly at Julian, who nodded, and averted his eyes from Adam's gaze.

As if he's hiding something, Adam realized.

"That's right," he said, and looked up at the café; Adam told him that he'd just missed Vikram, whose night off it was.

"Emma's still around," Adam said. "You could tell her."

"Sure..." Julian said, not sounding very sure at all. He looked at his watch. "Look, Adam, I'm going to be late. Do us a favour and tell Emma for me, will you?"

Adam smiled to himself: did Julian really think he was fooling him with his tale of a science project that he hadn't even started yet, with only three weeks to go before it was due to be handed in? Nevertheless Adam promised he would tell Emma so that they wouldn't waste their time waiting for him at the cinema.

"You're a mate, Adam," Julian said, relieved that he would be spared the embarrassment of having to lie to Emma. "I owe you one!"

"Any time," Adam said, and, as Julian made to go, he stopped him and asked: "You're just supposed to be meeting Jackie, Emma and Vikram at the movies, yes? No one else?"

Julian frowned, wondering why Adam was

suddenly so interested in who he was due to be meeting that night. But Adam had seen the looks that passed between Jackie and Vikram, and could see things in a much clearer light than could Julian.

"That's right – just me, Jackie, Emma and Vik," Julian confirmed, and, taking another look at his watch – "My God, I'm going to be so late!" – he made his goodbyes and raced out of the ice rink.

Emma came out of the girls' changing rooms, her skates slung over her shoulder, just as Julian left the hall. She joined Adam by the barrier; Adam was stroking his chin thoughtfully, and when he saw Emma, his face lit up...

"Was that Jules I just saw running out of here like a bat out of hell?" Emma asked. "I've never seen him run that fast except on the football field!"

Adam said it was. He smiled sympathetically at Emma. "He's just been in to say that tonight's cancelled," he said. And then Adam took a deep breath, as though lying was something he wasn't accustomed to, and said: "Something about a project he's got to hand in. He told me to tell you that Jackie and Vikram can't make it either..."

Emma's face fell. "I was so looking forward to that movie as well!" she said.

"You can always see it another time," Adam told her.

"Just my luck," Emma said miserably. "Stood up by my three best friends! Thank goodness I haven't got a boyfriend – or he'd stand me up too!"

Adam laughed and patted Emma on the back. "I

can't see why any boyfriend of yours would ever stand you up," he said. "You're pretty, intelligent and great fun to be with."

"No, I'm not," Emma protested, even though she felt a little buzz of pleasure at being told how pretty she looked by a guy as gorgeous as Adam. *Even if he is only being nice to me!* she added. "And besides, I'm fat."

"No, you're not."

"Yes I am," Emma insisted. "Compared to someone like Linsey, I'm enormous!"

"So stop comparing yourself to her then," Adam said sensibly. "Not all boys fancy pencil-thin, empty-headed bimbos, you know!"

That shut Emma up, and there was an awkward pause, before Adam said: "I've got a lesson to take, but after that I'm going to be free for the rest of the evening. Your evening's been called off, so why don't you hang around and then we could go around the ice a few times? Maybe we could go for a coffee at Slinky Jo's?"

Emma shook her head. "I can't afford any more lessons, Adam," she said sadly, choosing to ignore the ice-skating teacher's final suggestion. Why would he want to go out with her? she asked herself, as a wild hope sprang in her breast.

"And I'm not offering lessons," Adam said. "We can just go ice-skating – with a little bit of determination, Emma, you might even begin to enjoy yourself!"

Vikram wiped a tear away from his eye, hoping that Jackie hadn't noticed. They were sitting side by side in the movie theatre, having decided that they couldn't wait any longer for Julian and Emma to turn up; and Vikram had decided that what he called the "decided slushiness" of the movie they were watching perhaps wasn't so bad after all.

"Aha! Caught you!" Jackie giggled, a little too loudly, ignoring the protests of the couple sitting behind them. "You're a bigger softy than I am!"

Vikram gave her a friendly punch in the ribs, and continued to watch the movie, the tale of a nineteenth-century farm girl forced to choose between two men. He found it strangely moving, and by his side Jackie's bare arm accidentally brushed against his. The hairs on his arm stood up on end, as he became aware of Jackie's warmth next to him. She moved her arm away, but he could still feel its presence there, as though he had been branded with a mark that nothing would ever remove. Vikram shifted uncomfortably in his seat, crossing his legs, and trying to focus all his attention on the screen.

And how could he do that when sitting next to him was a girl who was a hundred times more beautiful than the heroine on the screen?

He turned and looked at Jackie, who was watching as the movie's heroine lost her beau to the wiles and machinations of the local scarlet woman. The actress playing her looked a little like Linsey, Jackie decided.

Suddenly Jackie was aware of Vikram looking at her in the dark, and she turned, smiled at him, and then returned to watching the film.

Jackie's eyes were bejewelled with tears as she watched the events on screen, and Vikram had an almost irresistible desire to reach out and gently dry them, and to run his fingers through her fine blonde hair. Jackie always complained about how unmanageable her hair was, and about her split ends – *whatever they are!* Vikram thought – but to him her hair seemed beautiful, as fine as gossamer and as golden as summer sunlight.

What the hell am I thinking of! Vikram thought angrily to himself. *She's the girlfriend of my best friend!*

He turned back to the screen, folding his arms as if to contain within him the emotions that he was finally admitting to himself. And as he turned his eyes away from Jackie, Jackie looked at him, and wondered why the normally so cheerful Vikram was frowning. He was troubled by something, of that she was sure, and she would have done anything in the world to unburden him of his problems. She sighed, and resumed watching the film.

They stayed like that, staring ahead at the movie screen, in silence, each of them alone with their own thoughts, until the credits rolled up on the screen and the movie drew to a close. The lights came up (but not as quickly as Vikram's hand which wiped the tears from his face before Jackie could see), and they stood up to go.

In the narrow aisles of the local cinema, Vikram found himself placing his hand on Jackie's back as he ushered her out of the seats. It was the most natural thing in the world to do – something

Vikram had done hundreds of times before – but now he froze, and drew his hand away.

It was raining outside, a soft summer shower, and Vikram unfurled his umbrella to protect them from the rain. Jackie hadn't brought hers, so she hooked her arm around Vikram's, pressing herself close to him so that she would be protected by the umbrella.

"That was a wonderful film," she said. "Emma and Julian will be so mad that they missed out on it!"

"It's odd that neither of them rang up to cancel," Vikram said, as they started walking down the road.

Jackie shrugged. "Who cares?" she said. "I've had a wonderful time with you, Vik."

"Yes, so have I..." Vikram said, and looked down at Jackie. *Just friends, and that's all.* And why did he not believe that any more? "Where to now, Ms Taylor?"

"If we were with Julian, we'd probably all go off to a posh bistro or restaurant," Jackie said teasingly.

"What d'you think I am, made of money?" Vikram feigned outrage. "It's a cappuccino at Slinky Jo's – if you're lucky!"

"Then Slinky Jo's it is!" Jackie decided, and she walked off down the rain-swept streets, arm-in-arm with Vikram.

Just friends, and that's all.

"Do you remember when we were kids, Vik?" Jackie reminisced. "Whenever there was a big storm and it started to thunder, I'd climb over the fence and into your dad's garden shed. It was your little 'den', and I always knew that you'd be there."

Vikram chuckled at the memory. "I remember – you were always frightened out of your wits. And only big brave Vikram could comfort you!"

"Liar! You were as scared as I was – that's why you were in the shed in the first place, hiding from the thunder and the lightning!"

"Maybe I was a little bit frightened..." Vikram admitted with disarming candour.

"I knew that we were like each other, you see," Jackie continued. "And that I didn't have to pretend to you. Mum would fuss over me and tell me there was nothing to worry about. But you were as frightened as me, and that was good because I could look after you, just as you could look after me."

Just friends, and that's all.

"A couple of scaredy cats, that's what we were."

"And sometimes I even used to look forward to thunderstorms, because then I knew that I could be *there* for someone, and that they'd be there for me. We needed each other, y'see."

They walked on in silence for a few seconds, and then Vikram said: "You've got Jules now."

Jackie sighed – with what emotion neither she nor Vikram was quite sure – and rested her head on Vikram's shoulder. "Julian looks after me, buys me things, makes sure everything's all right –"

"Even holds your hand in thunderstorms, I bet," Vikram said, attempting to make a joke of it.

Just friends, and that's all.

"But he never lets me look after him," Jackie said. "He never lets me pay for meals – unlike you, for instance."

"Hey, even with the job at Blades, I'm still on the breadline!" Vikram laughed. "If anyone's offering, this guy will take any free meals that are going!"

"And I bet he wouldn't have cried at the movie tonight the way you did," she said.

"That wasn't crying!" Vikram claimed. "That was merely an altruistic and noble attempt on my part to comfort a sobbing female in her hour of crisis, and make her feel comfortable in her great distress!"

"Yeah, and the rest," Jackie gloated. "For all your bravado, in my mind you're still the frightened little boy in his dad's shed –"

"Just don't spread it around, OK?" Vikram said. "I don't want anything to harm my reputation as an all-round all-purpose jock!"

"I wouldn't dream of it," Jackie said, and cuddled up closer to him.

Just friends, and that's all.

"Besides, until you learn to ice-skate you're not all-round and all-purpose!" she added. "And from your performance on the ice a couple of weeks ago, I don't think you ever will be!"

And that's when I knew, thought Jackie. *That's when I knew that you needed me. That's when I knew that I needed to be needed too.*

"The Leaning Tower of Pisa has a better sense of balance than you, Vik!" she said.

"Please woman, spare my blushes," Vikram said flippantly, at the same time deciding that he didn't quite like the turn the conversation was taking. "And less of the thunderstorm stories too! I don't want to be reminded of my days as a snotty-nosed, spotty kid!"

They stopped walking, and Jackie looked up into Vikram's dark eyes. "You're certainly not that now, Vik," she murmured.

"Jackie, I..." Vikram did not know what to say.

Just friends, and that's all.

He looked nervously about, at the passers-by walking briskly past them, more concerned with getting out of the rain than the conversation between two friends sheltering under an umbrella; he glanced over at Slinky Jo's across the road, it's candle-lit tables glowing warmly and invitingly; he looked at anything, in fact, except at Jackie.

Vikram was suddenly aware of Jackie's hand as it reached up towards his stubbled chin (even though he had shaved earlier that evening), and made him turn round to face her.

"Jackie..."

Just friends, and that's all.

It was inevitable, as certain as the night giving way to day, the sea rushing to shore, just two people finally following the dictates of their hearts. Vikram lowered his face to meet Jackie's and they kissed, a long, deep and passionate kiss, as they both acknowledged the feelings they had for each other that they had never before dared express.

Jackie felt the rough touch of Vikram's stubble against her cheeks, and ran her fingers through his dark raven curls, and down around his strong and muscular neck. She swayed with him, as if they were dancing, and not standing sheltered under an umbrella on a busy and rainy street.

That world of rain, of dirty wet pavements and of passers-by no longer seemed to exist for them. Vikram and Jackie: there was nothing else. There was no Adam, no Emma, no Linsey and certainly no Julian to intrude upon their happiness.

Vikram smiled, and caressed Jackie's soft cheeks, outlined her chin with his fingers, as gently as if he were handling prize porcelain. He had lowered the umbrella and the rain fell down on him, plastering his hair to his head, and leaving tiny raindrops lingering on his long dark eyelashes. To Jackie, Vikram appeared as some wild and beautiful creature of the deep, a handsome sea-god risen from the ocean.

They kissed again, more urgently this time, and Vikram held her tightly to him, as he nuzzled her neck, burying his face in her hair. And then he seemed to tense, and pulled back from her. He stood there for a long while, staring into the face of the woman he knew he loved. Jackie could see the love written on his face plain for all to see; she could also see the guilt and the fear.

"Nonono," he said, and shook his head. He released Jackie from his embrace.

"Vikram, what's wrong?" Jackie asked, and reached out for him. Vikram recoiled at her touch.

"We can't," he said, almost to himself. "We mustn't – it's not right..."

"Vikram, I love you," Jackie said. "I never knew before now. You were always around, the boy next door; I could never appreciate what was always under my nose..."

"You're my best friend's girlfriend," Vikram said, and his voice was breaking with emotion. "Don't you see? There's no future for us."

"But..."

"Do you love Julian?" Vikram asked, and he made no attempt this time to hide the tears which were already welling up in his eyes.

"Vik, I don't know..."

"I can't betray him," Vikram said. "You don't understand. We're mates, he's the guy I play football with, go out drinking with."

"Vik..."

"Let's just forget tonight, shall we?" Vikram said. "Pretend it never happened."

"But we won't. And it did."

"We're friends and that's all we are," Vikram said coldly, and turned and walked down the road, the rain concealing his tears which were now flowing freely.

Just friends, and that's all, Vikram had thought.

And now friends no more.

Just two broken hearts.

PART TWO

10

What followed was a living hell for Jackie, long weeks of bleakness and despair. Unable to admit to herself that she loved Vikram, she now tried to avoid him, as if not seeing him might make her ignore and then forget the longing for him which gnawed at her heart, a pain eating away at her soul. Torn between her love for Vikram and her feelings for Julian she didn't know which way to turn.

And it was so hard to avoid Vikram, for, in her efforts not to see him, she threw herself into her ice-skating at Blades; which was, of course, where Vikram was working. And every time she circled the ice she found her eyes looking involuntarily up at the window of the café, hoping that Vikram would be there, watching her.

At times he was, and when he caught sight of her looking at him, he would turn away, and return to his work, and chat distractedly to the adoring girl behind the counter who wondered why it had been weeks now since she had last seen Vikram smile that irresistible smile which turned her knees to jelly.

Jackie's ice-skating was improving daily now, and Adam was pleased with her progress. He had a special routine already worked out for her, he told her, and, even though she had had to cut down on her training because the winter term had started, he was sure that she'd be in fine form for the Christmas gala.

Dancing on the ice with Adam felt good, and Jackie could relax in his arms like a child cuddling up to her favourite brother. The two were becoming good friends, now that Jackie realized that there would never be any passion between them. She had been a silly fool all those weeks ago, Jackie now knew. And if she had been so mistaken in the feelings she had had for Adam why couldn't she have been wrong about her feelings for Vikram also?

She had tried approaching Vikram to discuss their situation, but whenever she had entered the café he had turned away, or immediately found an urgent job to carry out. Even when they met by chance at Slinky Jo's he had found some excuse to leave shortly after she had joined him and their other friends at their table. And when Jackie had shrugged philosophically and turned back to Julian, or Emma or Adam, to hide the sadness she felt, she failed to notice the look of anguish on Vikram's face as he took one final look at her before venturing out into the night.

“Boy, Vik’s so moody these days!” Julian said, after one of these encounters.

Emma nodded. “You’ve noticed it too?” she asked. “I’m worried about him. But when I’ve asked him what’s the matter, he’s snapped my head off!” She turned to Jackie. “What do you think is up with him?” she asked.

Jackie toyed with her cup of double espresso. “Me? I’ve really no idea,” she lied, and reached out for Julian’s hand under the table, as if that physical expression of her affection for Jules might take her mind off Vikram. She remembered there had been a time in the summer holidays when she had recoiled from Julian’s touch. Now she needed him there; and yet it was an act of desperation that was without any passion.

Julian pressed her hand lightly, and then withdrew his. “It’s the start of a new term,” he said.

“So what?” Emma asked. “It’s we three who are going back to college, remember! Lucky old Vik’s taking a year off!”

“He’s probably going to miss you two,” Julian said. “After all you won’t be coming to Blades quite as regularly as you have been doing.”

“Look, can we all stop talking about Vikram!” Jackie erupted. “If he wants to walk around looking miserable then that’s up to him, isn’t it?”

She stood up angrily, and in doing so, knocked over her cup of espresso. She cursed, and raised a hand to her brow, to soothe away the headache she knew was going to come any second.

Julian was suddenly all concern, and he put his arm around her shoulder. "Hey, Jackie, are you OK?" he asked.

"I'm fine!" she said, although at least to Emma it was patently clear that she wasn't. Julian, however, seemed to be convinced, and he returned to his seat. After a few seconds, wondering whether she should just rush out into the street after Vikram, Jackie sat down as well.

Julian beckoned to their waitress for the bill, and Jackie reached for her bag. Julian shook his head, and placed his hand on hers, preventing her from opening her purse.

Jackie sighed. "Julian, you paid for the last coffees, and the ones before that, and that meal two nights ago," she protested.

"It's my pleasure," Julian said airily. "Nothing's too good for you!"

"But..." Jackie said weakly.

"We're seeing so little of each other lately," he said. "It's the least I can do."

"I understand – your studies," Jackie said, and across the table only Emma noticed just how embarrassed Julian had suddenly become. Jackie was too concerned with asserting her own independence to notice the worried look in her boyfriend's eyes. "So let me pay, OK?"

Jackie sighed her assent: she knew she was fighting a losing battle. While Julian sorted out his change with the waitress, Emma groaned and stood up shakily.

"Look, guys, I'm feeling a little faint," she said.

"You are?" Jackie asked. Emma didn't look ill at

all; indeed for the past few weeks there had been a rosy glow in her cheeks and a happy spring in her walk. That was when she had seen Emma, of course; recently she seemed to have been keeping rather a low profile. They often used to meet up in the evenings at Slinky Jo's for coffee; now Emma was spending more and more time away from their regular haunt. If Jackie had not been so concerned with her own troubles, she might also have remarked that she was seeing less of Adam in the evenings too.

"Yes, I am," Emma said, and exchanged a conspiratorial look with Jackie. "I think I'd better go to the bathroom. Are you coming?"

"Sure," Jackie said, and stood up to follow Emma into the bathroom.

When they had gone, Julian smiled at the waitress who had brought them their bill. "What is it about you women that you always have to go to the loos in pairs?" he asked.

"It's so we can talk about you men in private," she giggled.

"And what do you say about us?" Julian teased.

The waitress – she was really very, very sexy, Julian decided – tapped the side of her nose. "Wouldn't you like to know!" she said.

Julian smiled at her and turned on his charm. "Well, maybe you should let me know sometime," he suggested.

"Sorry, we girls don't like divulging trade secrets to the weaker sex," she said in a friendly manner. "And besides I think your girlfriend might have something to say about it if we did!"

Julian chuckled, but there was a suggestion of regret as he turned his eyes away from the sexy waitress, and to the swing doors through which Jackie and Emma had gone on their way to the bathroom.

"Oh, yeah, my girlfriend," he said. "I forgot..."

"OK, what's the big deal?" Emma demanded as soon as they had walked into the Ladies'.

"'Big deal'?" said Jackie, and checked her complexion in the bathroom mirror. "I don't know what you mean. And besides I thought you said that you were feeling ill."

"That was just a lie to get you on your own, and away from Jules," Emma said. She glanced approvingly at herself in the mirror: she seemed to have lost a few pounds in the past few weeks. "What's happened between you and Vikram? Have you fallen out over something?"

"I don't know what you mean," Jackie said, and now started to examine an imaginary blackhead.

"Don't give me that!" Emma said. "Every time your name's mentioned he comes over all moody and withdrawn. And what was the matter with you just then – biting our heads off simply because we were talking about Vik?"

"It's just that I think there are more important things to discuss than Vikram's moods," Jackie said.

"Well, I don't think there are, Jackie Taylor," was Emma's reply. "He's my friend. So are you. And I don't like it when two of my closest mates suddenly look as if they can't stand the sight of each other!"

"It's not like that, Em," Jackie said wearily. "If anything it's the exact opposite..." She bit her lip: she had said too much.

Emma stared at her friend for a moment: a few things were starting to become clear. "Jackie," she said softly, "what is there between you and Vikram?"

Jackie paused for a moment, and then realized just how much she had been hurting over the past few weeks, keeping her secret to herself, going through all manner of torments to deny to herself and to her closest friends the reality of her love. She wanted to climb to the rooftops and shout it to the whole world: she loved Vikram, and she would love him for as long as there was breath in her body!

"It started a few weeks ago when Vikram and I went to see that movie," she began.

"I remember," Emma said. "Adam apologized to me the day after. He said he must have got Jules's message all wrong, and thought that the entire evening had been cancelled." Emma smiled to herself, remembering the first night she and Adam had gone out together; she would die if she couldn't tell someone about it soon, although Adam had advised her to keep quiet. After all, Betty Crabtree might frown on Adam seeing her outside "working" hours and his skating mothers might get so jealous of him spending time with her rather than with their beloved daughters, that they might stop the lessons in a fit of pique. Emma urged Jackie to continue.

"Well, after the cinema, we sort of..."

Emma didn't need to be told anything else; her face fell. "Jackie, you've been cheating on Jules!" she said.

"No, I haven't," Jackie retorted. "We kissed – and that was all... But Emma, it felt so right, so natural, so different from what I have with Julian. It felt as though Vik and I *belonged* together."

Jackie closed her eyes and involuntarily shuddered with delight, remembering Vikram's firm masculine body against hers, recalling his deep passionate kisses and the raindrops which lingered on his eyelashes.

"Jackie, you can't lead both of them on," Emma said.

"Don't you think I know that! Don't you think that I'm terrified of hurting either of them," Jackie snapped. "But every time I'm with Jules I keep finding myself thinking of Vik ... but he won't have anything to do with me!"

"He's scared," Emma realized.

"Scared? Of what?"

"Scared of losing his best friend," Emma said. "If Julian found out there'd be all hell to pay. You've seen how possessive he is of you, calling you his 'little girl', buying you all those presents, constantly making sure you're all right..."

"Jules is so sweet, and I really appreciate everything he does for me," Jackie admitted.

"And maybe he's also scared of commitment," Emma said. "Boys are funny like that; they'll run around with as many girls as they can, but when things start to get serious they go all cold on you."

"Vik doesn't run around with the girls. Jackie said. "He's never had a girlfriend before."

"Just a wife-to-be," Emma said darkly. The arranged marriage Vikram's father wanted to set up with Lakshmi wasn't something they usually talked about. Jackie and Emma had decided it should be a taboo subject, ever since Julian had confided in Jackie and she had told Emma.

"Vik won't marry that girl," Jackie stated categorically. "He's told us so."

Emma stroked her chin thoughtfully. "You know, this might explain Linsey's behaviour over the past few weeks," she said.

"Linsey?" Jackie had been successfully trying not to think of the sex-bomb of Blade's ice rink.

"Remember how she made a play for Vik when she first started coming to the rink?" Emma asked, and Jackie nodded.

"It's hardly surprising," Jackie said. "He is the sexiest and most handsome man in the place." She smiled wryly to herself: only a couple of months ago she hadn't even noticed Vikram's good looks; now they seemed to be part of that beautiful centre around which her entire life revolved.

"And then she suddenly left off," Emma continued. "Linsey may be like a cat on heat, but she's no fool. If a guy isn't going to be interested in her – because he's in love with someone else, for instance – she's not going to make a laughing stock of herself over him. She's the kind of girl who doesn't like to appear a failure, so she'll just look elsewhere."

"Like with Adam?"

"Adam?"

"Remember how she always used to show off whenever he was around?" Jackie said.

"Do I ever." Emma's voice was frosty as she recalled Linsey's stunning performance on the ice, and her suggestive remarks to Adam. Adam had certainly appreciated the performance; she hoped that the suggestive remarks had been a different matter. "And you're right, she has left Adam alone recently... She must have realized that he's a lost cause too as far as she's concerned. Maybe he's gone and got himself a girlfriend we don't know about yet?"

Emma was lost in reflection for a few moments, and there was a secret smile in her eyes; how she longed to tell Jackie her secret! She turned her attention back to Jackie.

"You have to sort it out with Vikram; you two can't carry on like this any longer," she advised her. "Tell him that that kiss meant nothing, that it was just two friends who went a little bit farther than they should have."

"But it wasn't nothing," Jackie protested. "It meant more to me than anything in the world. I would give anything to feel Vikram in my arms again..."

"You can't love two men, Jackie," Emma said. "Maybe Vik's doing the right thing, staying away from you."

"You can't mean that!"

"You're his mate's girlfriend," she said. "How do you think you'd feel if your best friend stole Jules away from you?"

"I'd..." Jackie began, and then stopped. How would she feel? Angry? Outraged? Betrayed?

Or relieved? Because then the field would be clear for her and Vikram?

"Do you love Vikram?" Emma asked.

A pause. "Yes, I do," Jackie said finally. "I never realized it before – but I've loved him ever since we were kids and he was the boy next door."

"And do you love Julian?"

"He loves me, Em."

"That's not what I asked," said Emma. "Do you love Julian?"

Another pause, slightly longer this time. "Yes, I do."

Emma shook her head sadly. "You can't love both of them, Jackie. This is the real world not some fairy-tale romance. You have to choose – for your sake, for Vikram's, and for Julian's."

Jackie was close to tears now. "But whatever choice I make, I lose out. If I pick Vikram then I'll have lost Julian as a friend, and Vik will have lost his best mate. And if I stay with Julian, then I'll never see Vik again. I can't stand losing either of them, Em!"

"You must make your decision, Jackie," Emma said. "Like I said – this is the real world!"

11

As the new term got under way, Jackie found herself far too busy to think about Vikram, or even about ice-skating as she threw herself into her college work. For a while things seemed to be going smoothly – she and Julian were getting on very well, helping each other with their course work (although his medical studies meant that their dates together became fewer and fewer). When they did get together, they had a good time, almost as good as they had had in the days before Jackie started noticing Vikram.

Yet Vikram was always there at the back of her mind, and if she had thought that staying away from Blades would make her forget the handsome young Pakistani then she was very much mistaken.

Wherever she went there seemed always to be some reminder of him; his favourite records were still being played over the PA system at Slinky Jo's; his favourite noodle soup was still on the menu at the sushi bar they all used to frequent; and of course Vikram himself was still working at Blade's, watching her as she skated with Adam on the ice, but never once coming near her, and only giving her the briefest of welcomes whenever he did see her. It was as if, by keeping as far away as possible from her, he would somehow conquer the feelings that Jackie knew he had for her.

Julian was aware that something was troubling her, but, as his studies were taking up more and more of his time, the subject was rarely broached when they did meet. He still continued to treat her like a princess, of course, and whenever he was forced to cancel a date Jackie always knew that the following day there would be an expensive present waiting for her by way of apology.

"A penny for them?" Adam asked one night as he skated up to Jackie who had been watching him from the barrier. He kissed her on the cheek.

"It's nothing," she said, and looked across the ice to where Linsey was performing one of her usual spectacular double axels. Linsey was wearing a floppy sweatshirt and jeans, similar to the ones Jackie was wearing: it was a marked change from the brash and tight Lycra cat-suits she had been wearing only a few weeks ago. Linsey had mellowed somehow, and didn't seem to be chasing the boys any longer – or at least not the ones who came to Blade's.

Maybe she's found a boyfriend now, Jackie thought, although she had never seen Linsey out alone with a boy; she realized that she'd seen less and less of the sexy skater on the ice too.

That puzzled Jackie for a moment until she remembered Vikram saying that Linsey was a science student at the local tech down the road; she supposed that now, in the initial run-up to her mock A-levels, Linsey would be just as busy as the rest of them.

Adam put his hand on Jackie's shoulder. "Who are you trying to kid?" he said. "You've been looking miserable ever since our lesson finished half an hour ago."

"I guess I'm worried about the Christmas gala," Jackie said.

"You'll be fine," Adam reassured her. "You're one of my best students: you'll knock 'em dead in the aisles."

"I'll probably fall flat on my face!" Jackie joked. "I've never skated in front of an audience before – I bet I'll be terrible!"

"Believe in yourself," Adam reminded her once again. "You do want to be in the gala, don't you?"

"Of course I do," Jackie said. "At first I thought it was only because I wanted to prove that I could be just as good as people like Linsey over there. And because –" she coloured.

"And because you thought you fancied me?" Adam laughed, and Jackie joined in.

"But now it's because I enjoy it so much, all the freedom, with no one in control but myself!"

"That's the spirit!" Adam cheered. "Always follow your heart. And always keep in control."

"Yes."

Jackie's eyes were drawn instantly up to the café, which was in semi-darkness. She'd never stayed so late at Blades before, but she knew that Vikram was usually there alone at this time, cashing up for the night.

Adam looked at his watch. "Jackie, I'm meeting Emma later down at Slinky Jo's," he said.

Jackie smiled: Adam had been seeing a lot of Emma recently. She wondered if anything was going on between the two of them, and then remembered just how radiant Emma had been looking recently: surely that was proof enough?

"Come along with me," he urged. "We need to talk anyway."

"About what?"

"Blades is going to be closed for a few weeks, for resurfacing, and re-icing," he told her. "It'll re-open at the beginning of December just in time for the gala. We'll have to find another rink for you to practise on."

"What about Vikram?" was Jackie's first thought. "Is his job going to be safe?"

Adam assured her that it would be, and walked off to the boys' changing rooms. As he did so, Linsey came off the ice and made her way to the girls'. She flashed a smile at Adam, and even nodded a hello to Jackie. Linsey had changed from the bitchy man-chaser of only a few weeks ago into someone who was much more subdued, at least whenever Jackie was around: and "subdued" was a word that Jackie had thought could never be applied to Linsey.

The ice-rink was empty, and eerily silent now that the PA system with its steady stream of chart pap had been switched off for the night. The overhead lights faded one by one, until the only illumination left was a stream of white coming from the café window. Slowly, Jackie climbed the stairs, and pushed open the door.

Vikram was sitting at one of the tables, poring over the till receipts and counting the cash he had taken during the evening session. From the piles of screwed-up balls of paper in front of him, it seemed that the former A-level maths student was having a major problem in getting the takings to balance. As the door creaked open, he looked up to see Jackie standing there.

"Vikram, we have to talk," Jackie said.

Vikram shook his head. "We've got nothing to talk about," was his awkward reply.

"We've lots to talk about!" she countered.

"Not now, Jackie," he said, and returned to his calculations. "I have to work."

"This is important," she said firmly and sat down opposite him. She took the pen from out of his hand, and pushed his till receipts to one side, so that he was forced to look at her. She placed his hand in hers, took a deep breath, and said:

"I love you, Vik. I don't care about Julian, I don't care about what anyone else thinks, I love you with all my heart."

Vikram's lips trembled and, from the look in his eyes, it was clear that all he wanted to do was to take Jackie in his arms and hold her like he'd never let her go.

"We've had all this out before," he said, a pained expression on his face. "You're the girl of my best friend."

"For heaven's sake, Vik, I love you!"

"What could I give you?" he said. "Julian's rich, he's good-looking –"

"So are you," Jackie insisted, and stood up and walked to his side of the table. "The handsomest, most caring boy in the world."

"He's got a great career ahead of him as a medical student and then as a doctor," Vikram said, and twitched uncomfortably for a moment when Jackie went behind him and put her hands on his shoulders. Slowly she began to massage the tense muscles of his neck, easing out all the stress and pain inside him. He could feel her breath on his neck, and he closed his eyes.

"Don't you think that it hurts me to deceive Julian, to fall out of love with him?" Jackie asked. "I love him, and I'd do anything to spare him any pain... But in the end all that really matters is you and me, Vik..." She buried her face in his neck, and kissed him there, smelling his freshly-washed hair and drinking in his scent. Julian had always smelt fresh and lemony, reminding Jackie of clear-running country streams; Vikram's scent was far earthier, far wilder, the tang of the storm-tossed sea, or the excitement of wild, unscaled mountains.

Vikram shuddered, but did not say a word. Instead he stood up, turned around, and kissed Jackie passionately on the lips. Jackie melted into his arms, knowing that here was her space, here was where she truly belonged. She felt her head spinning as Vikram's strong masculine arms held her tight; she felt the salt taste of his tears on her tongue.

"I need you, Jackie," he whispered. "I need you like I've never needed anyone before. Ever since we were kids, ever since the thunderstorms... These past few weeks have been agony for me – wanting you, needing you, and knowing that I could never have you, knowing that you were in the arms of someone else, in the arms of my best friend..."

"I just want to be with you for ever," Jackie said. "For the rest of our lives..."

Vikram drew slightly away from her, as though he had come to some sort of decision. "So will you tell Julian?" he asked, and Jackie tensed.

"It's not the right time," Jackie said, her voice breaking. Why did she lack the courage to give up her boyfriend? She knew that she didn't really love him. So why couldn't she bring herself to tell him? "It's not that simple, Vikram," she pleaded.

"Yes, it is," Vikram said, and his manner had suddenly turned cold. "We both lose one of our best friends."

"It's not that," Jackie insisted. "Julian loves me. It would break his heart if he found out."

"And what about my heart, Jackie?" Vikram asked, and wiped a tear from his eye. "What does my heart count for in all this?"

"Please, Vikram," Jackie begged. "Don't make me choose between the two of you. Not now."

"Then when, Jackie?" Vikram demanded angrily. "Are you going to string both of us along for the rest of our lives like a coward? That's not what love is about. Love is about sacrifice, about being brave enough to make difficult decisions; it's about following your heart, about doing what you want to do, not what you think you should do."

"Vikram, I..." Jackie made no attempt to wipe away the tears which were flowing from her eyes. Why was Vikram putting her through this torment? Why was he suddenly being so horrible to her?

Because he loves me, she realized. *And I'm tearing his heart apart.*

"What is it with you, Jackie?" Vikram demanded angrily. "Sometimes I think you're worse than Linsey. At least she sets her sights on only one boy at a time. But you're teasing both of us!"

"That's a horrible thing to say!" Jackie said. "I love you!" *But I love you both ... and I can't bring myself to hurt either of you!*

"And don't you think that what you're doing to me is horrible too!" Vikram said. "Just a few minutes ago you were saying that I was the only boy for you. But will you ditch Julian? Oh no, you want the best of both worlds!"

"Vikram, I'm confused," Jackie said. "Don't try and make me out to be some sort of cheap tart... Julian makes me feel good, but it's only you who makes me feel alive. When I'm with you I know I could do anything. You never smother me like Jules, you let me be my own woman, you treat me as your equal."

"You have to give things up for love, Jackie," Vikram said. "If there's any future for us, you have to break up with Julian..."

"Soon," Jackie moaned. "I have to pick the right moment: I can't hurt him..."

Long uncomfortable seconds followed in which Vikram did nothing but glare accusingly at Jackie. Jackie looked at him through a mist of tears, and watched as his fists clenched and unclenched in an effort to control the storm of passions rising within him.

"Thank you, Jackie," Vikram said, in a strange tone of voice.

" 'Thank you'?" Jackie didn't know what Vikram was talking about. "What for?"

"For helping me to make up my mind," he said, and, with the tears streaming down his face, he turned and ran out of the café, leaving Jackie alone.

She stood there for a few moments, and then the door opened again and Emma and Adam walked in. They were by her side in seconds, as they saw the obvious distress on her face.

"What's wrong?" Adam asked and he pulled out a chair for Jackie to sit on. He looked at the table, taking in at a glance the pile of money and the unbalanced till receipts. "We've just bumped into Vikram running out of here..."

"What's happened, Jackie?" Emma asked.

Jackie buried her face in her hands. "I've just broken the heart of the one man in the world I really love," she said. "And now I know what I must do..."

12

It was several days before Jackie and Vikram saw each other again. Jackie had gone round to his house several times, but when his father had answered the door she had been told repeatedly that Vikram wasn't at home. It was a lie, she knew, because on the last occasion she had seen a light in his bedroom window, so it was obvious that he was trying to avoid her.

Nor could she see him at Blades. The rink had now closed for resurfacing, and when she went out with Adam or Emma to Slinky Jo's the waitress told her that she hadn't seen him for several days now.

Julian was also proving difficult to get hold of. His telephone seemingly either constantly engaged or switched to the answer phone. She had left several messages, stressing that it was important that they meet up, but so far he hadn't rung her back. For a shocked moment, she thought that Vikram might have told Julian about them, until she realized that no matter how angry and betrayed he might feel, Vikram would never do anything like that.

Due to the temporary closure of Blades, Jackie was now taking her ice-skating lessons at the rink on the outskirts of town. Several of Adam's pupils had followed him there, and Jackie recognized many faces from Blades, including Linsey's. When Linsey had seen her, however, she had immediately left the ice; *probably out on the hunt for some poor unfortunate male,* Jackie had guessed, and thought nothing more of it.

To take her mind off Vikram (and Jackie still wouldn't tell Emma or Adam exactly what had taken place between them in the café), Adam had given her some free lessons, spending most of his spare time in the evenings coaching Jackie on the ice. She was getting better every day, he told her, and when the gala took place in five weeks' time she would be the star of the show.

"Betty Crabtree always invites some talent scouts to the gala," Adam reminded her. "They could spot you."

"And do what?" asked Jackie. "Sign me up for the next Winter Olympics?"

"You never know," Adam said. "You'll be good enough to star in a Holiday on Ice show at the very least – with a little extra coaching from me!"

"Now I know you're winding me up, Adam! The only skaters they'll spot are little cutesy kids they can train up to competition standard!"

"No, I'm not winding you up," Adam said in all seriousness, and Jackie was uncertain whether to believe him or not. She was looking forward enormously to the gala, and training for it at least took her mind off Vikram.

After her lesson had finished she went into the women's locker room where she showered and changed. Adam's compliments had cheered her up considerably, and, as she prepared to leave the rink, she was whistling a cheery tune.

She turned the corner, and her life changed for ever.

She took things in slowly, little by little. Julian was there, partly turned away from her. He was as attractive and as innocent-looking as ever, and for a moment Jackie wondered what he was doing at the ice rink when she knew that he only ever went skating with Emma and herself. What was more, someone as conscientious and as hard-working as Julian should have been studying at home.

He was wearing a baggy green Chevignon sweat-shirt – Jackie remembered saving up to buy it for him last Christmas – and the colour enhanced his sandy hair which she always thought looked so cute when it flopped over his eyes.

Long, red-nailed fingers were winding through that sandy hair, stroking his neck. In Julian's arms, in the middle of a serious clinch, was Linsey, her lips pressed tightly to his, lips that Jackie had tasted time after time.

Jackie felt the whole world spin sickeningly around her as she finally took in the complete image of her boyfriend and Linsey in their treacherous embrace. She felt somehow removed from the scene, as though she wasn't really witnessing this betrayal; she broke out in a cold sweat, and leant on the wall to support herself.

Her lips quivered, as if wanting to say something, but no words left her mouth. Her eyes stared, wide-open and unblinking, at Julian and Linsey who still hadn't noticed her.

No tears appeared.

She had been a complete and utter fool, Jackie realized suddenly. While she had been agonizing over her illicit love for Vikram, not wanting to hurt Julian, he had been playing around behind her back.

And with this...

This slut!

Jackie remembered what Emma had told her about Linsey, that she never fought a battle she knew she would lose. When Linsey had discovered that Vikram was attracted not to her but to Jackie, she had given up on him, while swearing revenge on Jackie.

She had then set her sights on Adam, thinking that he and Jackie had had a thing going (as if everyone was as cheap with their favours as she was! Some people still lived by certain standards – Vikram, for instance!) Linsey had tried to impress Adam with her skating skills, and, when it was clear that he was more interested in Emma, she had gone for the biggest prize of all: Jackie's own boyfriend.

Several things became clear to Jackie. Julian's cancelling several of their recent dates – presumably to spend time with Linsey. She'd remarked that his skating had improved recently: presumably he had been here skating with Linsey.

The little gifts he would give her after each of their broken dates were obviously his way of easing the guilt, and to stop her asking too many questions. And they had worked – up until now.

Only a few months ago, if anyone had asked Jackie what her reaction would be if she caught Julian cheating on her, she'd always imagined that she would break down in tears, or fly into a white-hot outburst of anger. She did neither of these things. She felt neither anger nor resentment, neither sadness nor hurt. She felt elation, happiness.

And an enormous sense of relief.

Julian and Linsey were suddenly aware that they were being watched, and they turned round. Julian's face fell, and he quickly released himself from Linsey's embrace. Linsey smiled in triumph – and then frowned, as she realized that her evil little scheme had not had the desired effect on Jackie. Jackie's eyes were dry; for heaven's sake there was even the hint of a smile on her face!

"Hello, Jules," Jackie said, keeping her voice steady and emotionless. "Hello, Linsey."

"My God, Jackie!" Julian said. "I can explain!"

"I'm sure you can," Jackie challenged him.

By Julian's side, Linsey gave a nervous little cough. "Er, Jules, I'd better be going now," she said. "Somehow I think you two might have a lot to talk about..." And with that, Linsey left Jackie and Julian to confront each other.

"Jackie, I know how it must seem," Julian said. There was a wild and desperate look in his pretty-boy eyes; their assumed innocence might have fooled Jackie once, but no longer.

"I know exactly how it is, Julian," Jackie replied icily.

"Darling, I'm really sorry," he said, calling Jackie "darling" for the first time in many months.

"How long?"

"What?"

"How long has this been going on?" Jackie said. "How long have you been cheating on me with that person?" She couldn't even bring herself to utter Linsey's name.

"A few weeks..." Julian said. He gazed down at his feet, like a naughty schoolboy brought up in front of the headmaster, rather than a sneaky two-timer who'd just been found out by his lover. He remembered the first time Linsey had come on to him, and what a louse he had felt when he'd passed on the message that he couldn't make the movie because he had some homework to catch up on.

"I can't believe that you were kissing her here," Jackie sneered. "Practically right under my nose, in the ice-rink I train at!"

Julian looked nonplussed. "I didn't know you'd be here today," he said, as if that somehow made everything all right. "Linsey said you didn't practise today..."

That witch, Jackie thought. Linsey knew perfectly well that, in the run-up to the ice gala, Jackie trained at the ice-rink practically every day. Not content with stealing Julian from her, she wanted to rub salt into the wound as well, by making sure that Jackie would catch her and Jules in the act.

Julian raised his head, and looked up at Jackie. "Look, darling, I'll make it up to you – I promise."

Jackie gave a scornful laugh. "Like you did all those times before?" she sneered. "Little expensive presents to keep me sweet? And to think I fell for it, fool that I was! How many other girls have you been seeing behind my back?"

"Only Linsey," Julian insisted. "She was the first..."

"And to think I thought you loved me," Jackie said, and allowed the first hint of emotion to creep into her voice. "To think that I even worried myself sick over ever hurting you..."

Julian stepped forwards and took Jackie by the arms: she pushed him off, not in anger, but with an odd sort of weariness. When he spoke to her, there was pain in his words, and absolutely sincere regret.

"This isn't really to do with Linsey, Jackie..." he began.

"Oh, isn't it?" she said. "You should have been where I was standing!"

"C'mon, Jackie, face it," Julian said. "It goes back much further than that, doesn't it? We both of us know it, but we were each of us too cowardly to admit it."

"What do you mean?" Jackie knew exactly what Julian meant, but she needed to hear him speak the words out loud.

"There's been something missing in our

relationship for months now," he said. "The magic we first had is gone. We were young then – you were my first girlfriend, I was the first boy you'd ever been out with. Perhaps we were too young. People change and little kids grow up."

"Like Vikram..."

Julian ignored the comment. "I remember a time when I had eyes only for you –"

And I for you, thought Jackie, and for the first time a tear appeared in the corner of her eye.

"And then I started noticing other girls, started fancying them, and I always felt guilty because I was your boyfriend, and I didn't want to hurt you, because you seemed so faithful, never flirting with the other boys. And so I started thinking that maybe we were meant just to be friends, and not lovers... But I still couldn't bring myself to tell you; because I didn't want to lose you as a friend, I didn't want to break your heart..."

"I was going to tell you weeks ago," Jackie revealed, and now her eyes were brimming with tears. She noted, with some satisfaction, that so were Julian's. "Back when I wanted to take you out for a meal at a country pub, but you had to see that doctor friend of your father's."

Julian remembered, and also recalled how he had spent that night alone, rather than go out with Jackie. If only they had told each other, instead of carrying on with this ludicrous play-acting! All along they had been lying to spare each other's feelings; if only they had expressed what their hearts were feeling, if only they had told the truth! He experienced intensely once again all the guilt he had felt at lying to Jackie, cancelling dates because of "studying" when, in reality, he was seeing Linsey.

He attempted an ironic laugh. "I guess we've both been a couple of prize idiots, haven't we?"

"The biggest fools around," Jackie agreed.

"I loved you, Jackie," Julian said. "And I still love you as my first girlfriend, as a sweet and caring person, and as one of my best friends. But I'm not *in* love with you any more... Can you understand that?"

"Oh yes, I can understand that," Jackie said, and Julian was taken aback by the depth of feeling in her words. Jackie recalled Vikram's question to her: *You love Julian, Jackie. But are you* in *love with him?* Julian had made her realize what her answer was.

"I'm sorry you had to find out this way," he continued. "And that it had to be with Linsey: I know that you two don't get on..."

Jackie smiled. "I have a lot to thank Linsey for," she said, "even though she doesn't know it yet!"

"I don't get it," Julian said. "What have you got to thank Linsey for?"

"For finally showing me where my heart lies," Jackie said. "For finally bringing me to my senses."

And then Jackie completely bowled Julian over by kissing him on the cheek, no longer the kiss of lovers, but the kiss of the best of friends who have been through a lot together and know that they will remain friends for the rest of their lives.

"I hope you're happy with Linsey," Jackie said (although she suspected that they wouldn't be for much longer), "and now I have to go and track down Vikram!"

"Vikram?" Julian frowned, as a sudden suspicion dawned on him. "You mean – you and he..." He no longer knew what to think. Jackie and Vik together? Part of him felt betrayed. Part of him felt relieved that he and Jackie no longer had to pretend to each other. And yet another part was so glad that Jackie and Vik – his two best friends had found what he and Jackie never could.

"Yes, do you know where he is?" Jackie asked. "I haven't seen him for days."

"I talked to him on the phone the other day, arranging a five-a-side match," Julian said slowly. "He's been away – 'on business'..."

"Business? What sort of business?" Jackie asked. "Never mind. Is he at home now?"

Julian shook his head. "No. I agreed to meet up with him later at Slinky Jo's..."

"Then that's where I'm headed," Jackie said and started to move to the exit.

"Jackie, don't..." Julian pleaded, but Jackie had already gone. He ran after her, only to see her hop on the bus at the bottom of the road.

Julian cursed, and ran over to the car park. It was essential that he catch up with her before she reached the café-bar. Julian might not feel for Jackie as a lover any longer, but as a friend he loved her with all his heart.

And he didn't want that friend's heart broken.

* * *

Slinky Jo's was crowded at nine o'clock that night when Jackie arrived. Winter was drawing on now, and the place was usually full of people attracted by its warm and friendly ambience. She walked through the door – *glided* might have been a better word, as she was so happy that she felt as if she was walking on air – and looked around for Vikram.

She panicked for a moment, as he didn't seem to be there. A mutual friend was passing and Jackie grabbed her, and asked if she had seen Vikram. The girl, who had carried a torch for the good-looking Vikram for ages said, yes, he was here, in the small chill-out room at the back of the bar, where people went to escape from the noise and the bustle of the larger bar; and didn't she think it was such a waste?

Not understanding the girl's last remark, Jackie pushed her way through the throngs of trendies around the bar to the chill-out room. There were several tables there, at some of which couples were huddled in candle-lit conversation.

Vikram was sitting at a corner table; he was dressed in a loose-fitting black jacket, and matching trousers, and a white designer T-shirt. Jackie hadn't seen him looking so smart for ages.

Or so drop-dead gorgeous! she thought, and noticed that his normally unruly mop of raven curls had been combed and slicked back. There was a glass of orange juice in front of him, which was unusual, as he normally drank only coffees or bottles of designer cider whenever he went to Slinky Jo's.

He wasn't alone. Sitting at the same table, each of them cradling a glass of orange juice were Vikram's father and a smartly-suited, slightly balding Pakistani man, who Jackie guessed was about the same age as Vikram's father. Unconcerned by their presence, Jackie caught Vikram's eye, waved at him and then walked over.

"Hi, Vik," she said happily and leant over and kissed him full on the lips. "Listen, I have the most wonderful news!"

Vikram sat back and nodded over to the stranger. "Er, Jackie, this is Mr Patel," he said politely, all the time wondering just what Jackie was doing here and why she was looking so happy.

Hadn't she heard from Julian? Didn't she know?

"Hi," Jackie said, and wondered why the man's name sounded so familiar; a glimmer of doubt came into her mind but she chose to ignore it, and continued to look lovingly at Vikram. She wanted to take him in her arms, tell him how much she loved and needed him, and beg his forgiveness for all the hell she had put him through. Finally free of Julian, Jackie no longer felt guilt over her love of Vikram; all she knew was a wonderful sense of release, a marvellous, instinctive conviction that their life together was now about to begin, a life in which every day would be a hundred times better than the one before.

"Julian and I have split up!" she announced importantly, as though it was the most earth-shattering piece of news she could ever deliver. As, indeed, it was.

"I shouldn't think that is something to be happy

about, young lady," Mr Patel harrumphed, but Jackie paid no attention to him. As far as she was concerned there was only one other person in Slinky Jo's, in the whole of the universe in fact, who mattered now.

There was a wary gleam in Vikram's dark eyes as he took in Jackie's news. "You ... you told him?" he asked, and Jackie wondered why he had suddenly turned very pale.

"No, but I've found out that's he's going out with Linsey," Jackie said, blissfully happy. "Isn't that wonderful news, Vik? It means that there's nothing standing in our way now!"

"Vikram, who is this?"

Jackie turned to see a gracefully petite Pakistani girl approach their table; she'd obviously just returned from the ladies'. Her silk trousers and tunic, shot through with filigree lengths of gold, made her look very classy indeed; her noble profile, almond eyes, and sensual mouth marked her out as breathtakingly beautiful. For the first time Jackie noticed the fourth glass of orange juice on the table, as the girl took her place, in between Vikram and Mr Patel.

"Vikram, who is this?" Now it was Jackie's turn to ask the question.

Vikram looked mournfully at Jackie, and back at Mr Patel; then to his father who had remained silent throughout the conversation, an uncomfortable expression on his face; and then, finally, at the gorgeous woman sitting on his left.

"Jackie, this Lakshmi Patel," he said with a heavy heart.

"Lakshmi?" The name rang a bell with Jackie, a bell that tolled doom for her heart and happiness.

"My daughter," explained Mr Patel proudly. "And Vikram's wife-to-be!"

Vikram's wife-to-be.

Jackie wasn't hearing this; she refused to believe it. This was a nightmare, a cruel trick played on her by fate. It was the end of everything, the end of her future happiness, the end of her life together with Vikram.

And it's all your own fault, she realized. *If only you hadn't been such a stupid little coward, if only you had told Julian how you felt earlier and split up with him. If only you'd have given in to your passions. If only you'd have admitted to yourself that the person you love most in this world is Vikram. If only you'd done what you wanted to, rather than what you thought was right... If only... If only...*

Jackie looked at Vikram. "Your wife-to-be?" The words came leaden to her lips.

Vikram nodded, and there were tears of regret – and of raging anger – in his eyes. "We're to be married in the New Year," he said, his voice cracking with emotion. "It's all been arranged..."

For Jackie there was nothing more to live for. From the heights of happiness she had been blasted down to the depths of despair. The world dissolved before her eyes into a tearful blur, and she was only dimly aware of someone coming up behind her and taking her arm.

"C'mon, Jackie, let's go home," said Julian, who had just arrived at Slinky Jo's. "The car's outside."

Jackie looked at her former boyfriend through a daze, as he guided her through the crowds of happy, smiling people.

"You knew, didn't you?" she said.

"I tried to tell you," Julian said. "But you left the rink so quickly..."

"It doesn't matter now," she said. "Nothing matters any more..."

And after Julian had brought Jackie home, she threw herself on her bed and cried and cried until she thought that she could cry no longer, until she thought that she would drown in her own tears.

And then she cried a little more.

13

To admire and to love a boy from afar, and know that your love will never be reciprocated is a terrible thing. But to love someone and to know that he loves you; and to be faced with the terrible knowledge that you have lost him forever, entirely through your own fault, is too much for anyone to bear. Jackie withdrew into herself, as she tried to answer a whole series of whys.

Why had she never realized just how much she loved Vikram before? Why had she ever gone out with Julian, when the only man for her had been living so close by, the boy-next-door for almost fifteen years? And why, when the relationship between her and Julian had so obviously broken down, had she not called a halt to it, instead of letting it stagger on, and ruin her life? If only she had done that, she and Vikram would be together now – no guilt, no shame, no Lakshmi and no wedding scheduled for early January.

Why? Because she had been scared, frightened

of following her heart. She had been sensible, responsible, adult about the whole affair; and it was only now that Jackie realized that true love is never sensible, responsible, and adult. It simply *is*, a force as inexorable as the ebb and flow of the tide itself. Follow it, go with the flow, do as your heart and not your head bids, and you will eventually be washed up on the shores of some tropical paradise; fight it, try to resist the pull, and you will surely drown.

Jackie was drowning now, in a sea of regret and bitterness. Even comforting words from Emma and Adam (and Julian, who knew what she was going through, and towards whom Jackie felt no bitterness) didn't help her; all that got her through the next few weeks, as the first snowflakes started to fall, was her ice-skating. She threw herself into it with an almost maniacal obsession, as if the faster she sped around the rink the quicker she could escape the mocking ghost of those saddest words in the English language: *what might have been*.

So it was a further blow on the bruise when, only a week before the ice gala and Blades' re-opening, Adam came up to her one evening at their training rink.

"We're double-booked," he told her, gritting his teeth to keep his anger in check.

"Double-booked? What do you mean?"

"Betty, Miss Crabtree, called me into her office back at Blades this morning," Adam said. "It seems that a charity five-a-side football match has been booked for that same night."

"Don't be stupid," Jackie said, as she skated over to the edge of the ice. "I've heard of hockey on ice, but never football on ice."

"Remember we're resurfacing the rink," he said. "There's still no ice on it, and Blades is the biggest indoor venue in town – it would be ideal for the match."

"Well, it'll just have to be cancelled," Jackie said practically. "The ice gala's booked for one week's time: it has to go ahead."

"The charity match is being organized by a wealthy foreign businessman," Adam said. "In return for the use of the rink he's willing to give Blades a handsome donation."

"But tickets have already been sold for the gala!" Jackie protested. "And you said that some talent scouts are coming up from London!" She remembered Adam telling her how proficient she had become; for the past few weeks she had been entertaining the notion that maybe she was good enough, even at the grand old age of seventeen, to be spotted as a promising young player in the sport she loved so much.

Adam rubbed his thumb and forefinger together. "We need the money," he said sadly.

"There has to be a way around it," Jackie said. "The gala can't be cancelled – not after all the effort I've put in. Not after all those lessons I've paid you for. We've both worked really hard for this!" She rubbed her chin thoughtfully. "Can't the venue for the gala be moved?" she asked. "We could have it here, where we've been practising ever since Blades shut down." Adam shook his head.

"There has to be a way around this!" Jackie reasoned. "Who is this businessman willing to put up the money anyway?"

"Someone called Patel," Adam said: the name meant nothing to him. "I think he owns a chain of grocery stores or something like that."

Vikram's father-in-law. Or rather he soon would be, Jackie realized. For one wild, unthinking moment she wondered whether Vikram had had anything to do with the double booking, to spite her. And then she remembered that Vikram loved her, even though she had not seen him since the news of his wedding, and that he would never stoop to such a mean, low trick. In fact, there was only one person she knew who could ever be so unscrupulous and wicked.

"Look, how did this double booking happen in the first place?" she asked. "I thought Crabtree was too efficient to let something like this happen."

"It wasn't her fault," Adam said. "It seems that–" he hesitated a second, as if debating whether to spare Jackie even more bad news – "it seems that Linsey has been helping her out in the office in the evenings. It was her fault. A clerical error, so they say."

I'll kill her, thought Jackie. *The little tramp isn't content to ruin my love life – now she's trying to destroy my ice-skating life as well!*

"Then get Crabtree to apologize to Patel," Jackie said. "I'm sure he'll understand..."

"That's the other problem," Adam said. "One of Betty's favourites is playing in the football match. She doesn't want to let him down either..."

"Vikram?" She remembered how Emma had once said that the old dragon-lady would be putty in the dark-eyed boy's hands. It seemed she had been right after all.

Jackie missed school the following day: it was nearing the end of term and she was sure she wouldn't miss anything she couldn't catch up on during the Christmas holidays. For most of the morning she looked out of her front-room window at the snow falling in the road outside, waiting for Mr and Mrs Pandy, Vikram's parents, to come out of their house, get into their cars and drive off to work.

This was the easy part. The hardest thing then was to gather up all her courage and walk around to Vikram's house and knock on his door. There was no response, and she was about to walk away when the door creaked open.

Vikram was standing there, still in his dressing gown, which was opened to the waist, and which he quickly gathered around him when he saw Jackie standing there. His hair was still wet from the shower, and there was a small nick on his cheek where he had cut himself shaving: it made him look innocent and vulnerable.

This was the man she loved, she knew, the man she could never have. The man she had not seen for weeks in the flesh, and the man she saw every night in her dreams. The man without whom her life would never be whole; the man who was marrying another woman.

Taken aback, Vikram let Jackie into the house,

forgetting to shut the front door in his confusion.

"Vikram, you must give up the football match," she said, after he had led her into the living room.

"Why?" he asked in a monotone. He looked at her with eyes which seemed to bore deep down into her very soul; at the same time he kept his distance from her. It was almost as if he was scared, Jackie thought, as if he was terrified of the passion he might express should he let himself come any closer to her.

"It clashes with the ice gala," she told him.

"So?"

"This is my big chance, Vikram," Jackie said. "Adam says I'm very good. There'll be important people down from London, who might be able to give me some work. This is my opportunity to make something of my life, Vikram, it could be the start of something big."

"You'll be in the gala?" This was news to Vikram.

"Of course I am," Jackie said irritably. "Why do you think I've been taking all those lessons with Adam? I wanted to keep it a surprise until the night–"

"Why?"

Always these damn monosyllables! Jackie thought. *As if he's scared of what else he might say!*

"I don't know – to impress you, I suppose," she said helplessly.

Again: "Why?"

Jackie threw her arms up in frustration. "What's the point in hiding?" she said. "The football match and ice gala aren't the real reason I've come around this morning; they're just excuses. I've come round to see you, Vikram. We belong together. It's not too late – you can still refuse to marry Lakshmi!"

Vikram tensed, and his jaw clenched. "I can't do that," he said.

"Of course you can!" Jackie exploded. "For heaven's sake, the marriage has been arranged between your two fathers! You can't love her!"

"What do you know about love?" Vikram shouted, even though he was breaking up inside. "It's your fault we all got into this mess in the first place!"

"What do you mean?"

"You thought you loved Julian, when all the time he was carrying on with Linsey!" he reminded her. "If you had followed your heart, done what you wanted to, if you had found the courage to tell Jules, then we'd be together now!"

"You're a fine one to talk about following your heart!" Jackie countered. "I didn't see you following your heart. Heck, it was you who tried to stop our affair!"

"You were my best friend's girlfriend! I had a duty to Julian!"

"Forget your stupid masculine pride and loyalty for a moment!" Jackie shouted. She made a half-way successful attempt to calm down. "Look, for whatever reasons, we've both been too scared to give in to our emotions. You're even doing it now."

Vikram stared wildly at Jackie: he knew exactly what she meant.

"This is our last chance, Vikram."

"To do what?" he sneered. "To 'follow our hearts'?"

"Well, you're certainly not following your heart by entering into an arranged marriage with Lakshmi, are you?"

"Leave Lakshmi out of this!"

"She's the whole reason I'm here, you idiot!"

"If I marry Lakshmi, then that will be the seal on a business deal my dad wants to enter into with Patel," Vikram said. "Patel has promised to invest hundreds of thousands into Dad's business. It means he could expand his chain of shops. It could make him very rich indeed..."

"I love you, Vikram."

"And what do I get if I follow my heart, as you call it?" he asked rhetorically.

"You told me once that love was all about making sacrifices," Jackie said.

"If I follow my heart, my dad stands a chance of losing his business," he said. "Do I have to sacrifice my family for you, Jackie? Can you really be that selfish?"

Jackie didn't know what to say; he was right. Why should he give all that up for her? "Vik, I'm sorry..."

"I love you, Jackie," Vikram said. "And I'll love you till the day I die. But I love my parents too. And someday maybe I'll be able to love Lakshmi as well..."

"Vik ... we have to be true to ourselves..."

Jackie moved forwards and reached out for him. He turned away, but Jackie pulled him back, and drew him into her embrace. Their lips met, and they kissed a brief kiss; and then a longer, deeper one, the last kiss they knew they would ever share. When their lips parted, Vikram's eyes were wet with tears.

"If only, Jackie, if only..." he said, echoing her own earlier thoughts. He stroked her fine blonde hair with his hands. "I have to marry Lakshmi..."

There was a click at the door, and Vikram and Jackie drew apart quickly. Lakshmi and her father were standing there: they had let themselves in by the front door which Vikram had neglected to close. Mr Patel opened his mouth wide, speechless, but Lakshmi took in the situation at a glance, and stared icily at Jackie.

"I think you'd better leave – and now," she said, and she and her father escorted Jackie to the door, leaving Vikram alone with his thoughts.

14

"Well, Jackie, I don't know what you did, but congratulations anyway!" Adam said the following day, and planted a friendly kiss on Jackie's cheek. They were in Slinky Jo's, sharing a cappuccino with Emma, and sheltering from the heavy snowfall outside.

"What have I done?" she asked, nonplussed.

"Why, got the football match cancelled, of course!" he said. "Betty's just told me. It's been postponed to the week after next – and to a different venue. The ice gala can go ahead after all!"

"Vikram."

"What?"

Jackie stood up, and excused herself. She went to the phone at the back of the bar, and punched in a familiar number. As she waited for the connection to be made she drummed her fingers impatiently on the receiver. He had thought of her after all, she realized; to give her a chance, he had possible risked the wrath of his father and Mr

Patel by cancelling the match. She had to tell him thanks, if nothing else; and who knew what else she would tell him? But when the phone was answered the voice at the other end made her heart sink.

Vikram's father answered the phone, and when she asked for Vikram, he told her that he was out. His tone became even more frosty when he recognized her voice, and he informed her that no, he didn't know where Vikram was, and that he had stormed out of the house the previous morning after an argument. It was obvious from Mr Pandy's manner that the argument had been over her, and he put the phone down abruptly, making it clear that he wanted nothing more to do with her.

Jackie returned, ashen-faced, to her table, where Emma immediately asked her what was wrong.

"Vikram's vanished," she said, as she eased herself back into her seat. Her legs were shaking, and she felt faint. She took a sip of her cappuccino. "He and his father have had an argument."

"Over what?" Emma was all concern.

"Isn't it obvious?" Jackie said, and told her and Adam everything that had happened the previous morning. "He's running away from his marriage."

"But that's great!" said Emma, not thinking through the consequences of Vikram's actions. "He's cancelled the match for you, probably upsetting both his dad and Lakshmi's father along the way; and now he's not going through with the wedding. He's doing it for you! He's proving once and for all that he really does love you!"

"And by doing that he's risking losing the love of his family," Jackie sobbed. "I can't let him sacrifice all that just for me."

Emma took hold of Jackie's hands. "Jackie, you and Vikram belong together," she said. "You always have done since you were kids, first as friends, and now as lovers. You can't let anything else stand in the way of that love. Love is all that matters, nothing else. Things will sort themselves out, they always do..."

"But where is he?" Jackie asked. "If he's doing all this for me, then why hasn't he come to me?"

"Is there anywhere you think he might have gone?" Adam asked practically. "Any friends he might stay with?"

"There's Jules," Jackie guessed, and also gave him the names of some other friends.

"We'll try them first of all," he said. "And then we'll look in all the places he usually goes – the gym, the leisure centre. And in the meantime you must continue practising for the gala."

Jackie nodded. "I know, it could be my big chance," she said. "And after all, it's to give me that chance that Vikram cancelled the match."

"Ah, yes, that..." Adam said and blushed with embarrassment.

"Adam, what is it?" asked Jackie.

"I'm afraid I might have misled you a little on that one," he said shamefacedly. "You're good, Jackie, one of my best pupils ever. But like you said, you're too old now to ever make championship level..."

"But you told me..."

"I needed the money from your extra lessons," he admitted. "And then when I got to know you, and when I saw your confidence grow on the ice, I continued to tell you that because I saw just how happy it made you. I'm sorry..."

"So Vikram's done all this for nothing," Jackie said, and wondered why she felt no anger towards Adam, only a sad acceptance of the way things were. Would she have gone to see Vikram if she hadn't thought she had had a chance at the gala? And if she hadn't seen Vikram, would he still be going ahead with his wedding plans with Lakshmi?

It seemed that Jackie's whole life was cluttered now with deceptions and misunderstandings – from kidding herself that she still loved Julian when she should have done the brave thing and called it a day, to Julian's cheating on her, to Adam's little white lies about her skating abilities. If only everyone had been straight with each other since the beginning – if only everyone had followed their heart – none of this would have happened. Yet in the midst of this sea of confusion one thing shone clear and steady, like a navigator's star, or a lighthouse beacon, guiding the weary storm-tossed sailor home: her love for Vikram.

For the man she knew she could never have.

The day of the ice gala dawned, and Betty Crabtree was in a state of excitement, ensuring that the newly resurfaced ice was ready for the big event. Banners and decorations were festooned around the rink ("Making it look like a crazy and particularly naff Christmas tree," Emma had said in a superior fashion), and even the PA system had been given such a major overhaul that some of the muzak blaring out from it actually sounded half-listenable.

In fact the only cloud on Betty's horizon, as the hall began to fill with the ticket-holders coming in from out of the heavily falling snow, was the absence of Vikram. It had been a week now since the rink had re-opened, and ten days since he had disappeared from home, and still there was no sign of him.

Betty had replaced him as manager of the café with his assistant, and when Jackie had asked her if she knew where he might have gone to, she had said that he'd probably run off with some girl. After all, she must have seen just how good-looking and sexy Vikram was, and didn't she know that all the girls were crazy for him? She had no idea why Jackie had then burst into tears.

Jackie had contacted everyone who knew Vikram, but no one had heard from him. Even Julian claimed not to know where he was, although the guilty look on his face as he told Jackie this had made Emma suspect that he knew slightly more than he was letting on. She kept her counsel on that, though, anxious not to raise any false hopes in Jackie. But when she and Jackie had left Julian's house, Jules had picked up the phone and dialled a number. The conversation that followed had been heated.

Now Jackie was waiting in the changing room of Blades, dressed in a stylish all-in-one leotard, and wearing her skates, as she waited for the piece of music which was her cue to go out on to the ice and perform the routine that she and Adam had been working on for the past few months.

All around her, other excited skating pupils were talking nervously to each other, wondering which big talent scouts might be out there in the audience; in the first half of the programme, someone said, a couple of promising seven-year-olds had already been picked out for special praise. Others, of a more practical nature, like Jackie, just hoped that they wouldn't fall flat on their faces as soon as they stepped out on to the ice.

Jackie could hardly hear them: their excited chatter sounded like the buzzing of faraway bees. Not only her hearing was dulled: her whole body felt numb and cold. She could hardly feel her own limbs as she stretched and warmed up, before going out.

There was only one thing on her mind, only one thing which could make her forget this aching emptiness. Vikram. Vikram who had risked his father's wrath, who had sacrificed everything, just so that she could have her chance out there now on the ice. Vikram who had given her the greatest gift of all – not presents or jewellery or CDs, but the willingness to put her own happiness and success before his own. Vikram who had always been there for her, through their childhood together, through the thunderstorms, and now, even though he was far away, in her own heart. Vikram had sacrificed so much for her: how could she now go out and perform on the ice?

She creaked open the door of the changing room, and looked out on to the rink. A young boy and girl, dressed in spangles and frills, were coming to the end of their ice-dancing routine: Jackie was due on in less than a minute.

In the front row of seats she could see Emma and Julian who had come to watch her performance; Linsey was nowhere to be seen, which hardly surprised Jackie. She'd guessed that Linsey would soon tire of Julian, and she was sure that Linsey wasn't the sort of person to come to an ice gala and watch other people being the centre of attention.

She closed the door. If she had kept it open for just one moment longer, she would have seen a familiar figure sneak into the hall. Vikram took his place at the back of the rink, but not before Emma had spotted him. Emma nudged Julian and whispered something to him, but Julian just nodded and smiled knowingly.

The two young kids sped off the ice to tremendous applause (none louder than that from their own adoring parents), and Adam glided into the centre of the ice to announce the next performance. He nodded to the organist at the far end of the rink, who launched into a fanfare, which was Jackie's cue to step out. With an exaggerated flourish, Adam invited Jackie on to the ice.

Jackie didn't appear. Adam appeared flustered, and nodded over to the organist to play the introduction again, as, for a second time, he announced Jackie.

Still no Jackie. A dissatisfied murmur arose amongst the crowd. Adam, ever the professional, looked down at the clipboard he was carrying to check who was the next act on the list: a pretty nine-year-old, for whom he held great hopes. He skated over to the organist, and instructed him to play the young girl's introductory piece of music. Jackie Taylor was ill, he announced, and he was very sorry that he hadn't known before. Unable to leave the ice as the master of ceremonies, Adam cast an urgent glance towards Emma, who had already left her seat and was making her way to the changing room.

"Jackie, what the heck do you think you're playing at?" she demanded, when she found Jackie, sitting disconsolately on a bench, her skating boots unlaced and lying on the floor before her. Her face was white and her eyes were red with crying.

"I'm not going on, Em," she said.

"Why ever not?" Emma said. "You heard what Adam told you: you'll knock 'em dead!"

"How can I go on after all that Vikram's given up for me?" she asked. "He's sacrificed his family for me."

"What d'you mean?"

"If it wasn't for him the gala wouldn't have gone ahead," she reminded her. "How do you think he explained that to Mr Patel, his future father-in-law? 'Sorry for postponing the charity football match but the woman I love – not your daughter, of course, but this cute number from next door – wants to go ice-skating'?"

"But, Jackie –"

"The least I can do is give up my skating. The only reason I agreed to do the gala in the first place was to impress him. And now that he's gone there's no point any more..."

Emma took Jackie in her arms. "But Jackie that's what I'm trying to tell you if only you'd listen to me!" she said. "He's back! He and Jules spoke on the phone last night. He's come back to see you perform!"

"Vikram? He's out there in the rink?"

"That's right," Emma confirmed. "I saw him arrive about fifteen minutes ago."

Jackie leapt up and rushed past Emma, a wild look of delight on her face. She ran out of the changing room, ready to throw herself into the arms of the man she loved with all her heart.

And he wasn't there.

She looked all around the rink, at the happy, smiling faces of the spectators, but there was no sign of Vikram. At the back of the rink, one seat was empty, mocking her, telling her that once again she had been too late, once again her hopes had been dashed, once again happiness could have been hers and she had let it slip through her fingers.

Jackie fell into Emma's arms and cried and cried and cried.

15

Jackie walked from the rink, her skating boots slung over her shoulder, having refused Julian's offer of a lift home, wanting to talk to no one about her loss. To have been so close to Vikram and then to have lost him yet again was too much. And the laughing faces at the gala, every single one of them unaware of her loss, made her sadness even more acute; in the distance she could still hear the blaring music and the rounds of applause, which seemed to be laughing at her, taunting her.

The snow was falling heavily now, and she could hardly see for the blanket of white which lay before her eyes. She wrapped her coat around her for warmth: it seemed as though it was going to turn out to be one of the coldest winters for a long time. Even the small pond, which she always passed on her way home from Blades, had frozen over.

But no matter how cold the weather was it could

never match the coldness in her heart, the bleak emptiness she saw lying before her. A lump of ice had encrusted her heart, freezing it in its sub-zero grip, and only Vikram could thaw it. But she no longer knew where he was. He would certainly not be at his father's; Vikram's dad was a stern man who would not have taken kindly to his son having disobeyed his wishes; and even if he did forgive Vikram, she suspected that Vik would have been much too proud to return home.

She had been a fool all along, she realized. Why hadn't she listened to her heart? Why did she always have to do what she thought she ought to do? Now she had lost the one man in the world she wanted, the one man in the world who was her equal and who could make her whole.

"There are other boys," Emma had told her when she had fallen, sobbing, into her arms, but Emma was wrong. There was only Vikram, and, fool that she was, she had lost him for ever.

It was getting dark now, and she quickened her pace, taking the short cut across the park to her home. The trees swayed in the winter wind, their bare charcoal-black branches as bleak and fruitless as the life that Jackie saw stretching before her. On the edges of the park, lights from distant houses shone invitingly with a warmness that Jackie would never know again.

The winter would pass, Jackie knew, and the trees would bloom and bear fruit again. But her soul was in the grip of a terrible Ice Age that would last her whole life long.

The path took her past the frozen pond. It was

iced over more than she had ever seen it before. In other winters some local kids had tried to skate on its frozen surface, before being warned that it was too dangerous but tonight it looked strong enough to support any weight.

There was a scrunching sound behind her, and Jackie froze. Slowly she turned around, to see who was approaching her through the snow. She couldn't see clearly – the snow was falling too fast and thick – but she recognized the broad shoulders, the slim waist, and the long shock of curly black hair.

Vikram stepped forward, and, as he did so, the full moon came out from behind a cloud, suffusing his handsome, manly face with a silvery-white radiance. Snowflakes crested Vikram's hair like a crown of flowers, or a halo. He looked like an angel, returned from heaven, or an elemental earth-spirit in whose eyes burned a passion red and wild.

Neither of them spoke. They just stared at each other, lovingly, knowingly. There was no longer any need of words.

Finally Vikram spoke. "Dance for me, Jackie," he said.

As if in a trance, Jackie bent down and took off her shoes. Keeping her eyes fixed on Vikram – she would never take her eyes off him again, she vowed – she slipped her skates off her shoulder, and pulled them on, and walked over to the frozen pond.

As she had guessed, the ice was thick and firm, and there was no chance of it cracking. With

Vikram watching, she stepped on to the ice, and circled the pond, performing the routine she had learnt with Adam. But this was now no longer just a display of ice-skating prowess intended to please the crowds. Now she was playing for an audience of one, and the dance was nothing less than an expression of her love for Vikram. The moon illuminated her like a spotlight, and the sound of the winter wind rustling through the branches of the trees provided a greater musical accompaniment than any organ or tape could ever do.

When she had finished, she stepped off the ice, unlaced her boots, and replaced them with her normal everyday shoes. She walked up to Vikram – she still had not said a word – and there, with only the moon and the falling snow for witness, she embraced him.

He felt warm and comforting, and Jackie pressed herself against him, melting their bodies into one body, their hearts and souls into one heart and one soul.

"I love you," he whispered, "and I'll never let you go as long as we both live. It's taken me all my life to realize it."

Jackie still didn't say a word: she just smiled blissfully at Vikram, knowing that whatever happened now they would always be together. This winter's night had proved it. Vikram was her winter and her spring, her summer and her autumn, her very world itself.

"You didn't do your piece at Blades tonight," he said.

"How could I?" Jackie said. "How could I be so selfish when I knew what you'd given up for me..."

Vikram frowned. "But you've given up your chance of a career in ice-skating," he said, and Jackie shook her head.

"That was only Adam spinning me a line to get me to pay for more lessons," she said, and chuckled. "I've as much chance of being an ice-skater as you have!" She stroked his hair tenderly. "But you've sacrificed much more than me..."

Vikram frowned once more. "What do you mean?"

"Your father... Lakshmi..." she said, and wondered why Vikram was grinning so.

"Lakshmi's called the wedding off," he said. "She realized that it would never work – as long as I loved you. It seems that she saw what no one else – ourselves included! – could: that we belong together, now and for always!"

"But your father?"

"Lakshmi told Mr Patel that it was her decision to call off the marriage," Vikram said. "He and my dad are still going to go into business. Even though my dad isn't too pleased about Lakshmi's decision: we had an argument about it and I stayed with friends for a few days to think things over."

"And the football match? Wasn't Patel angry about that?"

"I told him that several of the players had come down with the flu, and that the match had to be postponed for a few days. It'll still go ahead, and he'll still raise money for his charity."

Jackie feigned a look of discontent. "And there was I thinking you'd told him that it was because the woman you loved wanted to show off her skating!"

Vikram laughed, and pulled her closer to him. "No way!" he chuckled, and then became deadly serious. "But the point is that I would have done. And if Lakshmi hadn't have called off the wedding I would have done – no matter what I would have lost: my father, my future, everything. That's what love is all about, Jackie: it's about devoting your whole being to only one other person, and forsaking all others. And that's what I'm offering you, Jackie – my entire devotion until the very end."

"I love you, Vikram," Jackie said.

"And I love you too," Vikram said. "And one wedding might have been called off; but another one can be arranged..."

And as they kissed again, on that cold winter's evening, with the snow falling all around them, the ice in Jackie's life finally melted.